R

"I've got to go on trying. My son's been through a lot, you know,"

niel said, placing his hand over hers.

y nodded. "Growing up without a mother isn't easy. I know that from my own experience," she offered sympathetically. "But you're a good father, and you and Richie will eventually work things out."

"Eventually," Daniel repeated dourly.

Joey shrugged, then bent to pick up their mitts and started back to the dugout for the rest of their gear. "We'd better not leave Richie alone too long, Daniel. If that kid of yours is half as smart as I give him credit for, he'll soon get bored waiting for us, hot-wire my car and head for the New Jersey Turnpike."

Daniel took the heavy canvas bag full of bats and mitts from her and hefted it onto his shoulder as they walked to the car. "Much as I'm sure you've seen enough of anybody named Quinn to last you a lifetime, Joey, would you go to dinner with me tonight? I'd really like to talk with you some more."

"About Richie, I suppose?" she asked, feeling her heart sink to her toes.

"About Richie," Daniel admitted, then added softly, "and . . . other things."

Dear Reader;

This year marks our tenth anniversary and we're having a celebration! To symbolize the timelessness of love, as well as the modern gift of the tenth anniversary, we're presenting readers with a DIAMOND JUBILEE Silhouette Romance title each month, penned by one of your favorite Silhouette Romance authors.

Spend February—the month of lovers—in France with *The Ambassador's Daughter* by Brittany Young. This magical story is sure to capture your heart. Then, in March, visit the American West with Rita Rainville's *Never on Sundae*, a delightful tale sure to put a smile on your lips—and bring ice cream to mind!

Victoria Glenn, Annette Broadrick, Peggy Webb, Dixie Browning, Phyllis Halldorson—to name just a few—have written DIAMOND JUBILEE titles especially for you.

And that's not all! In March we have a very special surprise! Ten years ago, Diana Palmer published her very first romances. Now, some of them are available again in a three-book collection entitled DIANA PALMER DUETS. Each book will have two wonderful stories plus an introduction by the author. Don't miss them!

The DIAMOND JUBILEE celebration, plus special goodies like DIANA PALMER DUETS, is Silhouette Books' way of saying thanks to you, our readers. We've been together for ten years now, and with the support you've given to us, you can look forward to many more years of heartwarming, poignant love stories.

I hope you'll enjoy this book and all of the stories to come. Come home to romance—Silhouette Romance—for always!

Sincerely,

Tara Hughes Gavin
Senior Editor

KASEY MICHAELS

His Chariot Awaits

Silhouette Romance

Published by Silhouette Books New York

America's Publisher of Contemporary Romance

To Kathleen Schlosser,
chauffeur *extraordinaire*

SILHOUETTE BOOKS
300 E. 42nd St., New York, N.Y. 10017

ISBN: 0-373-08701-2

First Silhouette Books printing February 1990

Printed in the U.S.A.

Books by Kasey Michaels

Silhouette Romance

Maggie's Miscellany #331
Compliments of the Groom #542
Popcorn and Kisses #572
To Marry at Christmas #616
His Chariot Awaits #701

KASEY MICHAELS

considers herself a "late bloomer," having written her first romance novel after devoting seventeen years to her husband, four children, Little League and the avoidance of housework. Author of five Regency novels, she has also published a non-fiction book about her son's kidney transplant under her own name, Kathryn Seidick.

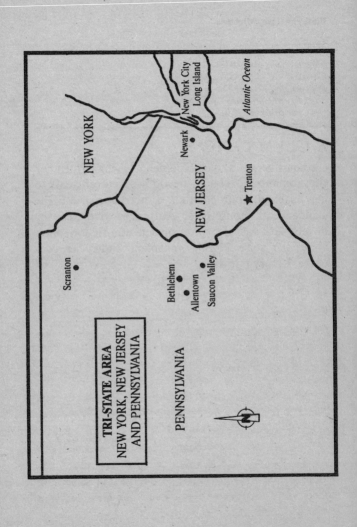

**TRI-STATE AREA
NEW YORK, NEW JERSEY
AND PENNSYLVANIA**

NEW YORK

Atlantic Ocean

New York City
Long Island

Newark

NEW JERSEY

Trenton

Scranton

Bethlehem
Allentown
Saucon Valley

PENNSYLVANIA

Chapter One

"Feel free to kiss me, Sis. You're looking at the genius who just landed us our first contract!"

"We have a contract? Right. *Sure* we do, brother mine. And on the way home a pink and purple pig waved to me as it flew by on the thruway." Josephine Abbott hung Esmeralda's keys on the white ceramic hook just inside the kitchen door of the century-old farmhouse, then plopped her weary body onto the nearest chair. "A contract! If that's supposed to be a joke, it's not funny. Rule number one, Andy—never hit a girl when she's down."

"You do look sorta beat, Joey," Andy remarked with the candor only a loving brother can use. "Esmeralda's not giving you any trouble, is she?" he asked, using his sister's name for the white stretch automobile that made up the entire assets of Abbott's Aristocrat Limousines. "Stay there, and I'll get you something cold to drink."

"Thanks, and no, Esmeralda's fine. Better than I am, actually. I've just spent three hours driving Mr. and Mrs. Reginald Putney III—of the New York and Newport Putneys, *dahling*—and their real estate agent around every blessed construction area within twenty miles. Not that they were too particular, you understand: just a five-bedroom Tudor, separate servant quarters, a six-car garage and a formal dining room large enough to hold *Maman*'s mahogany sideboard—and the Second Fleet, I imagine. And, oh yes, let's not forget the swimming pool and tennis court."

Andy gave a long low whistle. "They found a house like that around here?" he asked incredulously, twisting open a small bottle of orange juice and placing it in front of his sister. "I know we've got some good ones, but that sounds like a pretty tall order."

Joey lifted the bottle, tipped it toward Andy in a gesture of gratitude and then took a long drink of the ice-cold liquid. "That's the house they're going to *build*, Andy," she explained. "They were looking for 'just the correct piece of property' to serve as a setting for their architectural jewel." She slipped off her low-heeled black leather pumps and lifted her feet onto the facing seat. "All in all, bunkie, this is not a happy camper you're looking at right now. So no more cracks, okay?"

"Whoops!" Andy had pulled out the chair, not re-alizing his sister's feet were there, and quickly mumbled an apology as she was sent flying front to brace her hands against the edge of the table so that she wouldn't slide onto the floor.

"I love you, too," Joey grumbled, grimacing as she struggled to sit up straight once more.

"I said I was sorry about that, Sis." Turning the chair around so that he could straddle it, Andy leaned toward her, barely able to contain his excitement. "But I meant what I said when you came in, Josephine. No joke! We *have* got a contract." He spread his arms as if trying to show just how big the fish was that he had landed. "A real, honest-to-God, genuine, signed-on-the-dotted-line contract!"

Joey looked at her brother through narrowed eyes. He'd called her Josephine. Nobody had called her Josephine since she turned ten and developed a great, chin-crushing uppercut. He must be serious. She leaned toward him until they were almost nose to nose across the narrow kitchen table.

"Tell me about it, Andrew," she urged. "I'm all ears. And don't leave anything out, especially the part about how we got a signed-on-the-dotted-line contract—because we don't *own* any such animal. I wouldn't even know what to put in one, more's the pity."

Andy sat back and held out his hands, as if warding off an attack. "All right, all right, I'll start at the beginning. Remember that job I had Thursday, the day after you applied for the loan and came home moaning about not having any bona fide contract clients?"

"I said start at the beginning of the story—not at the beginning of time," Joey cut in as she set down the empty orange juice bottle. "I mean, Esmeralda's a car, but I don't think we need to hear the history of the discovery of the wheel, do we?"

"Yeah, well, I had to start somewhere, didn't I? Are you going to score points off me or listen to my story?"

"Now it's my turn to say I'm sorry," Joey answered sincerely. "Please ignore me, Andy. As I said, it has been a bad day."

"Apology accepted. Anyway, this guy, this Daniel Quinn, he moved here last month but still works in New York—in some humongous building on Sixth Avenue."

"How nice for him," Joey commented dryly, getting up to start dinner. Andy was a sweet kid, really he was, but he could take forever to get to the point, and she was hungry. She had to keep her hands busy, or else she would be tempted to go over and shake the story out of him. "You want frozen Chinese or frozen Italian? Lasagna it is. I'll make a tossed salad to go with it. Go on, I'm listening."

"Jeez, you're a tough audience," Andy said, shaking his head. "Now, where was I? Oh, yeah. This guy, Quinn, travels to New York three days a week and works the rest of the time at home. He's been driving himself back and forth, but he told me he thought he'd try a limousine service at least once to see if it would be worth his while to have someone else drive him. He spent the whole time reading, so I guess he wasn't working—I could see him in the mirror because the glass was down. Anyway, he called here today while you were out showing the Putneys all the local hot spots.''

''It's a good thing you want to be a singer and not a stand-up comedian, old chum. By the time you get to the punch line, the audience would have forgotten what the joke was about in the first place.''

Her brother stood and turned to leave the room. ''You're right, Joey, I'm a lousy storyteller. Never mind, it can wait until after dinner. Go wash your lettuce. I'll just watch television a while.''

''Andrew Carlisle Abbott, you get back in here this instant and finish your story!'' Joey called after him, laughing. ''This Quinn fellow—he's the one who wants a contract with us? For three days a week? For how long? What rate did you quote him?''

Andy grinned and tilted his head to one side so that his dark copper hair fell down over his forehead. ''You've heard every word I said, haven't you, Sis? I thought I'd lost you. It's for three days a week—Monday, Wednesday and Friday for six months—and I quoted him our usual weekday business rate, no discounts. He didn't even blink. We start Monday.''

''And the contract?'' Joey asked, suddenly feeling as if she were about to burst with excitement but wanting to hear the rest of Andy's story before she allowed her emotions to get the best of her.

''I took your car and went over to his place right away, before he could change his mind. He'd already had his legal department draw up a contract and we filled in the blanks together.''

"His own contract? I'm not sure I like that. I don't owe him my firstborn or anything, do I?"

"Relax. I'm a partner, right, as well as a college graduate and fairly literate? I *can* negotiate a simple contract. He's taking it back to his lawyers, and we should have it by Friday. We start driving him on Monday. He's a good guy, Joey. I wish I could drive him, at least for the first few times, but I've already got my plane and hotel reservations for tomorrow night, and I don't want to let the guys down. We've been planning this rafting trip for a long time."

"You did tell him about me?"

Joey had come up against male chauvinism more than once since starting the limousine service, so Andy knew immediately why his sister had asked the question. "Sure. Of course I told him," he answered airily, hungrily eyeing the salad makings. "Don't I always?"

Joey wielded the paring knife, neatly beheading a carrot. "How many tired woman-driver jokes did he crack before he finally ran down?"

Andy gingerly reached over her shoulder to steal a thick slice of green pepper. "Not a single one. He knows you're going to be his driver, and it's all right with him. Now, are you going to stand there all day or are you going to put down that potentially lethal weapon and give me a great big kiss for a job well done?"

Joey closed her eyes and let the joy race through her. Andy had done it; he'd really done it! Darn those Putneys for putting her in such a foul mood, and darn herself for being such a pessimist, even for a little while. She hadn't started Abbott's Aristocrat Limousines for the Putneys of the world. She'd done it for herself, and for Andy. And now, they might just get that loan for a second limousine. They were really on their way. Nothing could stop them!

She dropped the paring knife and turned to throw her arms around her brother's waist, hugging him tightly. "Andy, you darling, you're a genius! Three days a week in New York, with nothing to do but go to the museums, and walk in the park, and take in the Wednesday matinees, and—oh, Andy, you doll! How can I ever thank you?"

"You can loan me fifty bucks for that new oar," he suggested boldly, sensing his opportunity. "My old one's really beat, and you don't want your genius brother stranded up the Colorado for three weeks without his paddle, do you?"

"Done!" Joey promised, giving him another kiss before skipping over to the refrigerator and sticking her head inside. "There's got to be a bottle of wine left over from Christmas floating around in here somewhere. Andy, go out to Esmeralda and get the corkscrew from the bar. We've got something to celebrate!"

"Are you *still* working? It's six o'clock. I'm bored out of my skull. There's nothing to do around here."

Daniel Quinn laid the manuscript in his lap and peered over the top of his tortoiseshell reading glasses at the young boy who stood in front of him. His son's chin was hanging somewhere in the vicinity of his knobby knees. "Wow! That bad, huh?" he asked commiseratingly, shaking his head. "Where's Mrs. Hemmings?"

"In the kitchen," Richie Quinn replied, adding, "I was trying to explain how I could convert her recipes to the metric system, but she wasn't interested."

"You're kidding. Imagine that," his father supplied tongue in cheek. "I would have thought she'd be hanging on your every word."

"She threw me out, actually," Richie added, two small spots of angry color staining his pale cheeks.

Daniel's left eyebrow rose speculatively as he looked at his son. Richie's shoulders were slumped, his hands buried deep in the pockets of his plaid shorts, one sneakered foot kicking at a fringed corner of the Oriental rug, his carroty-colored hair drooping over his eyes.

At ten, Richie was tall for his age, but too thin. Too thin and too sad. Daniel couldn't remember the last time he'd seen the child smile or heard him laugh in real amusement. His son was also, at times, too damn smart for his own good. "Gifted," his teachers called it. There were times Daniel thought his son's intelligence was a curse, and his heart ached for him.

He sought to communicate, man to child. "Caught you elbow-deep in the cookie jar?" he ventured, removing his glasses and laying them on top of the manuscript. "That was always the reason I was banned from my grandmother's kitchen."

Richie raised his head and his freckles stood out vividly against his pale, child-of-the-city skin. His voice was weary, as if it was an actual effort to speak. "Mrs. Hemmings doesn't bake homemade cookies, Dad. She buys them at the supermarket. Oatmeal cookies. And some weird-looking things she calls health bars. Do you have any idea of the amount of chemicals and preservatives in that sort of thing? I won't touch them. Besides," he added softly, "I want chocolate chip."

"Hey, don't we all? But oatmeal's good for you," Daniel countered, placing the manuscript to one side unreluctantly—for it wasn't the author's most promising work—and getting to his feet. He refrained from commenting on the health bars because he'd never tried one and never wanted to, no matter how good—or bad—they might be for him. "Besides, it's almost dinnertime, isn't it? You don't want to eat now."

"I'm not hungry anyway. Just bored. I hate this place," Richie said, digging his hands even deeper into his pockets, and finally sounding like the child he was. "There's nothing to do around here. I still don't see why we had to leave New York for this dump. I miss Freddie."

Daniel walked over to a nearby table and lifted the lid of the ice bucket, just to see that Mrs. Hemmings had once again forgotten to fill it. He replaced the lid with a silent sigh. He hadn't really wanted a drink anyway; he'd just wanted something to do with his hands, something that would keep his face hidden from his son while he fought to get his sudden anger under control.

He was only partially successful, as he was unable to keep from remembering that, along with describing

Richie as "gifted," his teachers had also mentioned the word *precocious*. "Freddie! Always Freddie," he exploded, losing his temper. "Freddie's the doorman at our old apartment, Rich, for crying out loud. I want you to meet some new friends, some kids your own age."

"Freddie is my best friend," Richie argued to Daniel's back.

"Freddie snuck you into an off-track betting parlor and taught you how to handicap the horses," his father answered tiredly, for it was an old argument. "I'm trying to raise a son, not a racetrack tout. And there are plenty of kids in this neighborhood. I see them riding their bicycles all the time. You just aren't trying, Rich."

"Oh, yeah, sure. Bring that up again. You're just jealous because I won two hundred dollars after picking that long shot mudder at Aqueduct! And it wasn't fair to make me put it all in the bank!" Richie shot back at Daniel. He stomped over to the wing chair his father had vacated and flopped onto it, his long legs spread out in front of him. "Besides, I don't *want* to try. Why can't you understand that, Dad? I just want to go back to New York. This is nothing but a hick town full of boring kids. All the kids around here care about is riding bikes, and soccer—and *baseball*!"

Richie didn't know it, but he had just described his father's own happy, uncomplicated childhood. Daniel turned to look at his son, to look at the reason he had sold his exclusive Park Avenue condominium apartment and uprooted the two of them to Pennsylvania, the reason he had agreed to the grind of commuting to the city three days a week. Had he really expected thanks? The kid was miserable! "You're lonely, Richie, and I'm sorry about that," he began, repeating empty words he knew had already been said too many times. "But it's only been a month. Give it time. Perhaps in the fall, when school starts—"

Richie cut him off. "*School!* I'm not going to be stuck in this place when school starts," he declared hotly. "I'm going back to live in New York, whether you like it or not! And you know I can do it!" He turned and ran toward the staircase in the hallway.

"Rich! Richard Quinn, you come back down here right now! Richie, do you hear me? Oh, damn it," Daniel ended disgustedly as his son disappeared up the wide stairs to the second floor. "What's the use?"

Walking back over to the chair, he sat down, replaced his reading glasses and opened the manuscript once more, only to stare at it without really seeing the words. He had thought this move was such a good idea; getting Richie out of the city and into the open air, where he could experience a normal childhood. But it wasn't working.

"And that's the understatement of the century," he said out loud, closing the manuscript once more. Langley Books must have published a half dozen self-help books for mothers raising children alone, but he couldn't remember a single one directed at fathers raising a child in a motherless home. "Talk about your instant bestsellers," he mused. "I'd be good for a half dozen copies myself."

"What's that you say, Mr. Quinn?" Daniel looked up to see Mrs. Hemmings walking into the room, wiping her hands on her apron. "I've just come to get the ice bucket in case you want a drink, not that I hold with drinking strong spirits, you understand. Herbert, my dear departed husband, drank, and he's been dead a dozen years. There's a lesson there, don't you think?"

Daniel didn't bother answering, as he had quickly learned that Mrs. Hemmings asked a lot of questions, but was never really interested in hearing any answers. Besides, having already experienced the housekeeper's garbled logic firsthand, he decided that her "dear departed" Herbert had probably been run over by a beer truck. "Has Richie been bothering you, Mrs. Hemmings?" he asked instead.

The housekeeper's expression went from grim to grimmer, and she shook her head. "That's one unhappy lad you've got there. You know what I mean?"

"Yes, Mrs. Hemmings," Daniel said on a sigh, knowing that Richie's unhappiness had more to it than the move to Pennsylvania. It also had a lot to do with his Grandfather Langley. "I know exactly what you mean."

Joey strode confidently along the brick sidewalk of the Plexiglas-canopied Hamilton Mall—an ebony-haired bundle of unlimited energy neatly packed into a slim, five-foot-nothing frame. Still humming garbled snatches of a hit song, she approached the broad intersection at Seventh Street and the tall Soldiers and

Sailors Monument that stood squarely in the middle of the street.

Stopping on the cement traffic island in the middle of the intersection to wait for the Walk sign to turn green, she jauntily saluted the bronze statues guarding the monument. It was a practice she'd begun in her youth and stubbornly adhered to ever since, no matter how many times the policeman on the corner looked at her as if trying to judge her sobriety. Some things were just traditional.

The knife-sharp creases in her black pleated skirt fanned out around her knees as she resumed her walk, and she quickened her pace as she took a moment to glance at the slim gold watch on her left wrist. Although she was not tall, her legs were long and straight and the black leather heels she wore added almost four inches to her height. The policeman looked at her a second time, his expression openly admiring.

Automatically reaching up to smooth the foaming lace neckcloth that cascaded halfway down the front of the black vest she wore over the crisp white long-sleeved blouse that completed her uniform, she smiled back at the officer.

Her mood was just too good to let anything bother her. It was June, the sun was shining, she had her health, and she had just walked out of the bank after submitting her request for a whopping loan and been given a fairly enthusiastic "we'll see" by the vice president in charge of ambiguous answers. But, as the man's "we'll see" was a lot better than the "you've got to be kidding, Miss Abbott" expressed by the loan officer she'd approached before landing the Quinn contract, she'd immediately decided that Abbott's second limousine was all but an accomplished fact.

It was still difficult for Joey to believe that she was the owner of her own business. She'd come back home to Allentown two years earlier when Andy graduated with honors from Lehigh University in nearby Bethlehem. Within hours of her arrival Joey had discovered that during her nearly two years as a jobless free spirit, her finances had declined almost to the point where she would have to start drawing on her principal.

She had also learned that Andy—with a degree in mechanical engineering in his back pocket—had no plans to take any of the positions he had been offered, but had every intention of becoming Pennsylvania's answer to Bruce Springsteen.

"Baby Andy," now towering over Joey by more than a foot, had obviously been expecting his wandering, carefree big sister to understand how he felt, so his surprise had been very real when she had looked up at him through the bright orange lenses of her oversize wire-rimmed sunglasses and declared flatly, "In your dreams, Sherlock!"

Andy had used every argument he could think of, but to no avail. Joey had been adamant. It was one thing for Andy to want to become a professional singer—but it was a horse of an entirely different color to think that he wouldn't have to find some sort of gainful employment while waiting for his big break to come along.

The inheritance from their father, added to that of their mother, who had died when Andy was only six, had been enough to keep a roof over their heads and pay their college tuition. But the remaining money, along with Joey's own savings and investments from her years with Ransom Computers, wasn't enough to give even one of them a free ride forever.

As much as she wanted to help her brother, Joey had known the two of them would have to find a way to put food on the table—and feeding Andy was no easy task! Joey had taken a deep breath and announced that both she and Andy had to get themselves gainfully employed—fast.

Going back to Ransom Computers had been out of the question. If there was one thing Joey had decided during her two-year hiatus it was that she wanted— needed—to be her own boss. A second decision, one that had taken her all of five seconds to make, was that she never wanted to see another computer spreadsheet or corporate meeting as long as she lived.

Andy, having told her that mechanical engineering wasn't nearly as glamorous as it was cracked up to be, had then suggested that they look around to find something more suited to the lives they wanted to live. "Of course," he had added tongue in cheek, "that might mean you'll be wanting us to drive tractor trailer trucks full of frozen french fries or something, considering that all you've been doing for two years is driving from here to there and back again."

Driving. Joey loved to drive. She loved the feeling she got whenever she was behind the wheel. She loved watching the scenery and the people go by. Since the first time she sat on her father's lap at the age of ten and "helped" him steer their ancient family station wagon along a deserted back-country lane, Joey had been fascinated with driving.

Andy had been nearly knocked off his feet as Joey launched herself into his arms, kissing him soundly on both cheeks. *Driving.* What an absolutely brilliant brother! What an absolutely brilliant idea!

And that, as she had just finished explaining to the vice president in charge of ambiguous answers, was how Abbott's Aristocrat Limousines had been born.

"Abbott's Aristocrat, because we call it AA Limousines for short and that makes us first in all the telephone directories," she had told the vice president with pride. "People have the tendency to begin at the beginning when looking in those books. We were going to call it Abbott American Aristocrat—for AAA, you understand—but we only needed two A's to be first."

Now, Joey thought as she headed left into the parking lot, all we need is *two* limousines. She waved to the parking lot attendant as she walked along the aisle between the rows of cars, then stopped beside her pride and joy, the long, gleaming white limousine she had affectionately dubbed Esmeralda. Opening the door, she picked up her black chauffeur's cap and placed it at a jaunty angle on top of her short, soft black curls before sliding behind the wheel and slipping her seat belt over her shoulder and around her small hips.

She took a moment to run her hands lovingly over the plush maroon velvet of the wide bench seat, then turned to look over her shoulder at the rest of the interior. The smoked-glass partition between the driver and passenger sections was in the lowered position so that she had a clear view of the "club room," as Andy called the area that held two facing velvet seats, a small drinks bar, television set, VCR and combination radio and tape deck. "All the comforts of home and then some," the salesman had said the first time Joey saw it, and she still had to agree.

The limousine was big, a stretch model, but it wasn't gigantic. She hadn't been afraid she couldn't handle a larger vehicle, but she had disliked the feeling that she was driving a bus. Esmeralda handled beautifully, and sat six in the back easily, which was more than enough room for her clients, who ranged from newlyweds to prom goers to society matrons to businessmen. Allentown, indeed the entire area, seemed to have a large appetite for limousines.

That appetite was growing, fed by the construction of Interstate 78, the highway that was rapidly bringing New York City within reasonable commuting distance. Daniel Quinn wasn't the only Saucon Valley resident commuting to the city. A building boom that had begun two years earlier was in full swing, with new housing developments and industrial parks springing up almost overnight and local real estate values climbing into the stratosphere.

Joey couldn't have picked a better time to go into business, and her business was growing right alongside that of the rest of the community.

For herself, Joey didn't intend to get too big—her memories of Ransom were still with her—but she would have been a fool not to take advantage of the opportunity that had somehow dropped into her lap. Andy's music career had begun to progress slowly but had not exactly skyrocketed him to the cover of *Rolling Stone*. So as long as there were two drivers available she couldn't see any reason not to add a second limousine. It only made good sense.

After paying the parking attendant she pulled into the traffic on Sixth Street, a small frown creasing her normally smooth forehead. If only she had something more concrete to show the bank than her past records and a few optimistic projections for increased revenue. She knew the demand for her services was growing; after all, hadn't she lately been turning down an average of three jobs a week? Being a free spirit was one thing, but money was still money!

"But now you *do* have a contract—thanks to Mr. Daniel Quinn, bless his heart—and by this time next week you'll have your loan!" she reminded herself as she slipped a recording into the tape deck and headed back toward Seventh Street and the drive home to nearby Saucon Valley.

Chapter Two

Early Monday morning Joey Abbott tooled Esmeralda down the narrow, twisting macadam road that only two years earlier had been bordered by a rolling, treed landscape almost devoid of development, admiring the sprawling houses and small estates that had been delicately carved into the countryside.

Every house was a reflection of its owner, whether it was a modern wood-and-glass multistory flight of fancy or an updated re-creation of some bygone era. Each home occupied at least two acres of land, kept as close to natural as possible, with hardly any trees having been sacrificed to open lawns.

Joey slowed the limousine to watch for the left turn she would have to make onto Olde Country Lane, then drove about a half mile before seeing the oversize mailbox with the name Quinn painted on it in black block letters. She turned in the long driveway that curved up the sloping front yard and parked Esmeralda in front of the mellow pink three-story Colonial, silently complimenting her new employer's good taste.

Sneaking a quick look in the rearview mirror, Joey pressed her lips together to smooth her Radiantly Red lipstick as she turned her head this way and that, making sure her hair passed muster. Satisfied that she was as good as she was going to get, she unhooked her seat belt and stepped out onto the driveway.

Hands on hips, she surveyed the area in front of the house, noting that the driveway returned to the street in a semicircle, while also branching off at the end of the house, probably leading to a separate garage. "Poor man," she said out loud, "roughing it like this in the boonies after all those bright lights in the big city."

She debated whether or not to ring the doorbell, checking her watch to make sure she was on time. Some people didn't appreciate having their doorbell rung at six o'clock in the morning, and Joey wasn't eager to meet Mrs. Quinn if she wasn't ready for company. She'd give Mr. Quinn five minutes to show up before searching for him, she decided. She reached into the limousine to pull out a soft white cloth, planning to keep herself busy polishing Esmeralda's already gleaming chrome.

She was squatted in front of Esmeralda's grille, careful to keep her uniform skirt off the ground, when a young male voice pointed out, "You're not Andy Abbott."

Joey turned to see a boy of about twelve sitting on his haunches next to her, glaring into her eyes. "Good point," she acknowledged, flicking the soft cloth lightly against his freckled nose before standing up. "And you're not Mr. Daniel Quinn, unless he's a child prodigy. Are you?"

The boy stood at the same time. He was taller than she was, although Joey silently determined that that wasn't much of a feat. Nearly everybody was taller than she was. The boy tipped his head to one side and asked, "Am I what? Daniel Quinn, or a child prodigy? Your question lacks direction. Always be specific."

Joey frowned, looking at the boy in consternation. "Oh, great. Everybody's a critic. Is your father home? You are Mr. Quinn's son, aren't you? Take the second question first, if that's all right with you."

"That's better," the boy complimented without cracking a smile. "That was reasonably lucid. Yes, I am my father's son and, yes, he is at home. My name is Richie. Richie Quinn. Now, who are you?"

Joey couldn't believe her ears. It must be all those vitamins kids are taking these days, she thought. She couldn't remember even *knowing* a word like *lucid* when she was twelve years old, let alone being able to use it in a sentence. He was very tall. Maybe he was a little older than she thought. "Richie, is it? How old are you, anyway?" she asked, curiosity getting the better of her.

"I'm ten years old, but everyone thinks I'm a lot older because I'm intellectually gifted," Richie informed her, clearly not intending to brag, but merely stating a fact. "I'm still waiting to hear your name, and what you're doing here instead of Andy."

"I'm Joey. Joey Abbott, Andy Abbott's sister," she answered quickly, realizing she had just been firmly put in her place. "You're tall for ten," she added weakly, almost apologetically.

Richie just shook his head. "Joey? That can't be your real name. A joey is a baby kangaroo. You must really be Josephine."

Fun was fun and all that, but enough was also enough! "And *you* must be mistaken," Joey supplied stonily, her eyes narrowing dangerously as she placed her hands on her hips and glared at him. "You may call me Joey, or Ms. Abbott, or Hey You—but don't you *ever* call me Josephine. Not if you want to live to see eleven."

Richie seemed to consider this for a moment, then brightened. "I don't think it matters what I call you, since I won't be seeing you again. My father won't allow himself to be driven by a woman."

"Wrong again, kiddo," Joey countered. "Your father already knows his chauffeur is a woman. Now, what do you say you run off and find him for me so we can get this show on the road. Not that this hasn't been fun, but I want to beat the traffic through the tunnel."

"Lincoln Tunnel?" Richie asked, his voice carefully uninterested. "I guess the buses go through there too—to the Port Authority."

"Yes, they do," Joey agreed absently as she heard the heavy white front door of the brick house opening, then turned to get her first look at her contract employer. "Oh!" she exclaimed in sudden shock, Richie and his comment quickly fleeing from her mind.

Daniel Quinn was quite a man, even at six-something o'clock in the morning. Tall, about the same height as Andy, he had broad shoulders and a narrow waist, as if he had joined that increasing group of executives who visited health clubs several times a week. His strides were long and confident as he came down the half dozen steps of the wide, curved cement porch, his head held high as his piercing blue eyes shot fiery bolts straight through her, figuratively nailing her black leather pumps to the driveway.

He was sleek and graceful, like a jungle cat, his tanned skin molded cleanly over the strong bones of his face. His double-breasted suit was flawless, midnight-blue with fine pinstripes; his shirt pristinely white; his tie the requisite conservative deep maroon worn by television news commentators and politicians all over the world.

He was, in a word, the corporate world's version of a hunk. *All the good ones are married,* she thought, immediately wondering why she had thought it. Joey swallowed hard and forced herself to walk toward him, her right hand outstretched. "Mr. Quinn, I presume?" she heard herself say, then stood uncomfortably as her hand was ignored.

"Who are you?" Daniel Quinn barked sharply, running his gaze up and down the length of her in obvious disbelief—and dissatisfaction. "You're not Andy."

He has more in common with his son than their last name, Joey thought sarcastically as she silently cursed her absent brother. Andy had said Mr. Quinn knew about her. Obviously there had been a breakdown in communications. "I'm Joey Abbott, Mr. Quinn. Andy's big sister."

"Joey?" Daniel repeated, looking toward the limousine and then back at her. "Joey's a man's name. Andy told me . . . I just assumed . . . that is . . . no! Absolutely not! This is totally out of the question! I hired a chauffeur, not a *chauffeurette*."

"Told ya," Richie offered in a low, singsong voice as he sidled past Joey to stand next to his father, before continuing. "I informed her that you won't care to be driven by a woman, Dad," he said, his childish voice now deliberately deepened for this man-to-man exchange. "I knew you wouldn't allow a woman to drive you through downtown traffic."

Daniel looked down at his son, feeling vaguely uneasy with this rare show of male togetherness. Usually Richie went out of his way to take the opposite side of any issue. "You don't think I'll be safe with a woman driver?" he asked the boy. His startlingly blue eyes narrowed speculatively. "Or have you just made a quick bet with Mrs. Hemmings that I won't allow it?"

Joey could sense a sudden tension in the air, a tension that had nothing to do with the fact that she had taken her brother's place as Daniel Quinn's chauffeur. "Look, I don't want to butt in here, but if we're going to reach the city before noon we should get on the road now. Give me a shot, Mr. Quinn, just one round trip. I haven't lost a passenger yet. Then, if you don't like me, we can see about making some other arrangements until my brother returns in three weeks. He's on vacation with friends in Colorado," she added, although why she was bothering to explain herself she couldn't quite understand.

Without waiting for an answer, she walked up to Daniel, relieved him of the bulging leather attaché case he was holding and quickly deposited it in the backseat of the limousine. Purposely holding the door open so that Esmeralda's plush maroon interior beckoned invitingly, she prompted, "Mr. Quinn?"

Richie moved closer to Joey, and his father overheard him whisper out of the corner of his mouth, "Nine to five he cans you on the spot."

"You're on, bunkie," Joey whispered back at him, winking. "Fifty cents too steep for you?"

"Hey," Richie said, surprised. "You're not half-bad—for a girl!"

Daniel decided it might be time to teach his son a lesson. "Be right with you, Ms. Abbott. Richie—pay the lady tonight, out of your allowance." He placed his hand firmly on Richie's shoulder and guided the boy out of Joey's earshot. "Put a candle in the window, kid," he whispered, once more reaching out to the boy on a level he hoped would have some effect. "Do you think she sits on a pillow to see over the steering wheel? I'll be back around seven-thirty—if I live that long."

Richie's face was carefully, maddeningly blank. "If you say so, Dad," he answered, shrugging so that Daniel's hand was left suspended in midair. "And if I'm still here, we might even have dinner together."

Daniel opened his mouth to call his son back, but the boy had moved with surprising speed, running up the steps two at a time and disappearing into the foyer. Daniel sighed, suddenly feeling very old and very tired. *Tonight,* he decided silently. *We'll talk tonight, when I get home. This has gone on long enough.*

Walking over to where Joey was standing, still with one hand on the open door, he brushed past her with only a mumbled "thanks," and allowed her to close the door behind him. He reached for his attaché case and randomly pulled out an accounting spreadsheet. Maybe if he kept his attention glued to the pages he could fight off the nearly overwhelming urge to tell Ms. Joey Abbott to move over, and let him drive.

The highway wasn't too congested, with most of the traffic being caused by interstate trucks on their way to New York, but Joey knew that commuter-filled cars would be lined up ten deep at the tollbooth by the time they reached the entrance to the New Jersey Turnpike.

Her passenger had been unusually quiet for a first-time rider; most of her clients seemed eager to make friends with the person who quite literally held their lives in the palms of her hands. Aside from the obvious but harmless jokes about women drivers, clients most often discussed the state of the weather, their reason for hiring a chauffeur in the first place—some

of them actually embarrassed to be riding in such luxurious comfort—and wondered out loud how a "little
bit of a thing" like Joey could pilot a vehicle the size of
Esmeralda.

But Daniel Quinn hadn't said a word, even when
Joey lowered the tinted-glass partition to double-check
the address of his destination. She'd left the glass in the
lowered position for a few minutes, inviting conversation, then raised it, determinedly shoved a Learn Con-
versational French cassette into the tape deck and
practiced saying "Would you kindly direct me to the
nearest policeman."

Let him sit back there and read his stupid reports,
she thought, glancing in the rearview mirror to see his
silhouette outlined through the glass. *It's not like I
want to talk to the man anyway, unless it's to ask him
how he came to have a son like Richie.* "That kid's
something else," she said out loud, missing the opportunity to repeat after the instructor: "I am a lost
American. Would you please direct me to—insert the
name of your hotel."

Yes, Joey decided, Richie Quinn was quite a character—part boy, part man and part nasty little brat. He
was also intelligent, extremely intelligent—that she
could tell just from listening to him speak—but he was
still a child, and his emotional maturity hadn't quite
caught up to his superior intellect. He had the makings of a rare handful, and she didn't envy his parents
a bit.

Yet, she thought, conjuring up a mental picture of
the boy who had dared to correct her speech, he isn't a

happy child, for all his intelligence and material possessions. Joey would have been willing to bet that Richie had every toy known to man—and then some—and probably a computer as well.

It was Richie's paleness that bothered Joey most. Although he looked just like his father, with his bright red hair already showing signs of deepening to the rich chestnut of the older Quinn, Richie definitely lacked his father's outward signs of good health. How could a ten-year-old boy make it to the middle of June without acquiring at least a slight tan? It wasn't normal.

She stole another look into the rearview mirror. Maybe she should ask Mr. Quinn if Richie wanted to join the baseball team. The roster was full but, as one of the coaches, Joey could still find a place for him. The Quinns had only lived in Saucon Valley for a month, according to Andy; maybe they just hadn't had the time to search out an activity for their son.

Before she could talk herself out of it, and before she could remember Andy's warnings about poking her nose into places where it didn't necessarily belong—and might not be particularly wanted—Joey pressed the button that lowered the partition and called back to her passenger, "Has Richie found a team yet, Mr. Quinn?"

Daniel raised his spectacled eyes from the page he had been reading for the third time, wondering how this book from a rival publishing house could have made the bestseller list. It certainly wasn't riveting enough to keep his mind off the fact that he had somehow allowed himself to be torpedoed down a busy turnpike with a half-pint female behind the wheel.

"Team?" he repeated in confusion. "What sort of team are you referring to, Ms. Abbott? Sports? Richie doesn't care for team sports."

Joey took the time to shoot a quick look over her shoulder at her passenger. "Really?" she questioned, as if genuinely astonished, although she had already guessed as much. Richie seemed more like a loner than a joiner. "But aren't there any junior baseball teams in New York—in Central Park or somewhere? After all, with both the Yankees and the Mets in town, I would think every little boy would want to play baseball."

Daniel lifted a hand to adjust his reading glasses, horn-rimmed half-frames that had a tendency to slide to the end of his nose whenever he spoke. "I don't know why you would suppose that, Ms. Abbott," he returned stiffly. "Richie's into horse racing—or at least the odds-making end of it, as numbers fascinate him— but I can't recall his expressing any desire to become a jockey," he pointed out reasonably. "And shouldn't you be keeping your eyes on the road?"

"Well, excuse *me*," Joey muttered beneath her breath, "I guess that puts me firmly in my place." Raising her voice without turning her head, she explained, "I didn't mean to intrude, Mr. Quinn. It's just that I help coach a local team of ten- to twelve-year-old boys and girls whenever I'm free, and I thought it might be a good way for Richie to meet some of the other kids in the neighborhood."

Daniel shook his head in self-disgust, realizing that he had overreacted to Joey Abbott's obviously innocent and well-meaning overture. He was becoming defensive about his son—overly defensive—and was beginning to see criticism even when it wasn't there.

He had Wilbur Langley to thank for that, he knew, as Richie's maternal grandfather had been making the boy his personal project lately, pointing out all the child's supposed problems and offering his own totally unacceptable brand of solutions. Having Richie move in with him was Wilbur's latest brainstorm, and as far as Daniel was concerned, it easily topped the man's long list of unsuitable remedies to Richie's problems.

"Forgive me if I snapped at you, Ms. Abbott," Daniel apologized gruffly. "As a former Little Leaguer myself, I have to admit I was disappointed when Richie decided not to follow in my footsteps. Rich is just not very—um—physical."

"That's a pity," Joey said commiseratingly, silently wondering why the child should suddenly seem so important to her. "With his height he'd make our local basketball coach a very happy man. At this age they don't need to be experts—it's enough to have one tall boy he can camp underneath the basket to wait for rebounds. Oh, well, maybe you and your wife can convince Richie to at least give baseball a try." She peeked into the rearview mirror again, trying to see his expression. "It's worth a shot, isn't it?"

"Richie's mother has been dead for seven years, Ms. Abbott," Daniel informed her, his words clipped and cold even to his own ears. "I'm raising Richie myself, which is why we moved to your area in the first place. It's not easy, raising a child in the city."

Joey was aware of the increased tempo of her heart upon hearing that her new client was a widower. "I'm so sorry," she said automatically, ashamed of her real reaction. Although she felt badly for motherless Richie, there was no denying facts. Daniel Quinn was a very attractive man, and he had appealed to her on sight.

She fell silent, suddenly trying to remember the last time she'd looked at a man and found him interesting, attractive. She couldn't remember. Yes, yes she could. It was a long time ago, during her junior year in college. His name was Pete Williams and he had been a campus jock—majoring in football, willing coeds and, when the spirit moved him, political science.

Joey had been fascinated with Pete, mostly, she thought now, because he had been fascinated with her, but it hadn't lasted beyond the middle of their senior year. Pete had been what she had bitterly described as "a legend in his own mind," and she had eventually tired of the role of adoring handmaiden.

There hadn't been anyone since Pete. Joey had been too busy carving out a niche for herself in the corporate world, and her two years spent traveling the country hadn't lent themselves to forming any lasting romantic attachments. For the past two years she'd been fully occupied building up Abbott's Aristocrat.

Joey frowned. She was twenty-eight years old. The business was still in need of her undivided attention—

and there was Andy and his "career" to consider. At the rate she was going, she'd better prepare herself to be an old maid. Shrugging fatalistically, she comforted herself that she had at least not lost the ability to notice an attractive man when he landed in her backseat!

And Daniel Quinn was going to be her regular passenger three days a week until her brother returned from Colorado in three weeks. She smiled. Maybe there was hope for her yet.

Suddenly, a loud noise penetrated the well-engineered silence inside the limousine, a sound reminiscent of a pistol shot. "What the devil—" she exclaimed as the tractor trailer in the process of passing her in the left lane veered toward Esmeralda, forcing the limousine toward the shoulder of the road.

"Hold on, Mr. Quinn!" Joey shouted in warning, clutching the steering wheel with both hands. She shot another quick look to her left. She could see that the truck had lost the right-front tire on its cab, and the driver seemed to be fighting a losing battle with the balky steering and the heavy, shifting load he was hauling behind him.

A look to the right told her that orange-and-white-striped construction barrels lined the shoulder of the road, making the area too narrow and too dangerous for Joey to consider escaping the truck by turning that way. Quickly checking the rearview mirror, she saw a huge fuel truck riding her rear bumper.

She couldn't slam on the brakes, not unless she wanted to have Esmeralda turned into a big white metal pancake. She had been riding behind another large trailer truck, so there was no open space in front of her.

There was simply nowhere to go to get away from the out-of-control truck.

The driver of the truck in front of her, seeing her problem, tooted his horn and accelerated, trying to give her enough room to shoot over into the passing lane, ahead of the swerving tractor trailer.

"Oh, God," Joey breathed, understanding what had to be done.

It might work. If she could accelerate fast enough...if she kept her head and didn't turn the wheel a second too soon—or a moment too late...if the disabled truck didn't sideswipe the limousine first...if she could successfully thread Esmeralda through the very small eye of the needle that was the only patch of open highway left between her and sure disaster...it might just work.

All this and more raced through Joey's mind in a few precious heartbeats as she slammed the gas pedal to the floor—including random thoughts concerning the extent of her medical insurance and the realization that Daniel Quinn was being extremely quiet in the backseat.

Esmeralda responded to Joey's commands beautifully, the sleek limousine powerfully surging ahead of the disabled tractor trailer, then successfully threading the needle to safety with at least two inches to spare between it and the truck in front of it.

Joey watched in her rearview mirror as the disabled truck swerved completely into the lane she had just vacated, then limped to a stop half on the shoulder of the road. Her heart pounding, her mouth uncomfortably dry, she eased her white-handed grip on the steering wheel and beeped her horn in thanks as she passed the trucker whose swift action had given her the room she needed to pull off her evasive maneuver.

"That was—er—that was very *good*, Ms. Abbott," she heard Daniel say, his voice almost normal. "I thought we'd had it for a moment. Congratulations, and thank you. I saw my life passing before my eyes for a second back there, and I realized I have a lot more I want to do before I meet my Maker."

Joey laughed, happy for any excuse to release the tension of the past few moments. "You're welcome, Mr. Quinn, and I feel the same way," she responded happily, remembering it was just what she had been thinking about before the near accident.

"Daniel, Ms. Abbott," he corrected. "Now that we've practically decorated the same highway together, I think we can dispense with the formalities. I'll call you Joey, if I may, and I'll be happy to have you as my chauffeur for the next three weeks and beyond, if our schedules don't conflict. You're a very competent driver. I don't know if I would have reacted nearly so well."

"Well, thanks again—Daniel," Joey responded, smiling at him as she saw his face reflected in the rearview mirror. "I appreciate it—even while I wish I could have proved myself a little less dramatically. We'll be coming up on the tunnel soon," she went on; suddenly uncomfortable with their unexpected relaxation of formality. "You should be at work in another fifteen minutes."

"You know you're to pick me up again at five-thirty?" Daniel asked. "What will you do all day?" He made a face as he heard himself ask the question, wondering why he should care what she did. After all, entertaining his chauffeur wasn't his problem. "Surely you don't drive all the way back to Allentown?"

"Good Lord, no!" Joey answered happily, pulling up to the tollbooth for the Lincoln Tunnel. "But don't worry about me, Daniel. A person who can't find something to do in New York City doesn't deserve your pity. Today I think I'll walk around Forty-second Street and the theater district. Most of the theaters are dark on Mondays so it won't be too crowded."

"Sounds—um—delightful," Daniel remarked, secretly thinking he would be bored out of his mind within twenty minutes. He picked up the book that had slid to the floor during the course of their near accident and once more ignored his driver.

Chapter Three

Langley Books. How about that!'' Joey repeated out loud for the tenth time as she walked away from the security parking garage, her well-traveled purple high-top sneakers cushioning the soles of her feet from the hard New York City pavement. "I wonder what Daniel does there—and it's dollars to doughnuts he isn't the office boy."

Langley Books, she knew, was one of the largest publishing houses in the world, and one of the last still privately owned and not a part of a multi-imprint house or conglomerate. It was also one of the most respected and diversified houses in the industry, publishing everything from self-help and textbooks to romance, sci-fi and thrillers, both in hard cover and paperback.

Joey knew all about Langley Books. Oh, yes, she certainly did. After all, hadn't they turned down her query letter just three weeks ago, without so much as asking to see the manuscript?

One for the Road might have been Joey's baby, an outpouring of her innermost thoughts and personal observations during her years since leaving Ransom Computers, but to Langley Books it was just another rejected idea. "Not suited to our needs at this time," the printed form letter had read, and her brother, Andy, had quickly fashioned an airplane of the paper and launched it toward the wastebasket in the corner of the kitchen.

"Their loss, Joey, their loss," he had told her bracingly. "Just don't give up. It's a great book."

"This from a guy who hasn't read a word of it," Joey had replied, lifting her head from the cradle of her arms as she sat slumped at the table. "But thanks anyway. What bothers me is that they didn't even give me a chance. How are they going to know whether or not the book is good if they refuse to read the thing? This is the third publishing house to turn me down unread. If only I knew somebody with some influence—some clout."

"And now I do," Joey said out loud, not attracting any attention to herself, because hearing people speak out loud to nobody in particular on the streets of New York was as accepted as the never-ending traffic. "I know Daniel Quinn. Heck, I even saved the guy's life— in a manner of speaking. I wonder if he has any real pull at Langley Books. For all I know, he could be the head of the accounting department. The very *handsome* head of the accounting department," she amended, smiling in spite of herself.

"Mr. Quinn," a woman's voice said over the intercom, "I have Courtney Blackmun's agent on line one. He says he won't talk to anybody other than the publisher on this one. Something about Ms. Blackmun wanting a new press kit. Shall I say you're in conference and can't be disturbed?"

Daniel depressed the button and spoke into the small brown box. "It's all right, Mrs. Feather. I'll take it." Picking up the phone, he deliberately smiled, hoping the smile would show in his voice. "Harry! Good to hear from you again. How's the tour going? Did Courtney get the flowers we sent? I caught her kickoff appearance on that talk show last week. She was wonderful, as usual."

Quickly moving the phone away from his ear so that he wouldn't go deaf, Daniel depressed the button that would send Harry's irate shouts bouncing off the walls of the paneled office, then adjusted the volume of the speaker phone.

"How's the tour going?" Harry screamed. "How's the tour going! It's *not* going, damn it! What idiot found it necessary to put the name of Courtney's daughter's boarding school in her press kit? She saw it this morning and damn near took the roof off the hotel. She refuses to go on with the tour until she has a whole new press kit."

Daniel rubbed a hand across his mouth, silently acknowledging that somebody in the publicity department had made a major blunder. Courtney Blackmun deserved a little privacy. She was one of their top money-makers and her fourteen books had been best-sellers both in hard cover and paperback.

But Courtney could also be Langley Books' major pain in the neck. Demanding and autocratic though she was, her fame made her very valuable—while her carefully worded contracts made her impervious to editing—and she must be kept happy at all costs, no matter how it galled Daniel to bow to her sometimes outrageous demands.

"But Harry," Daniel pointed out rationally, "the press kits preceded this tour by a good month. Printing new ones now with her daughter's school name deleted would only call attention to it."

Daniel could hear Harry's world-weary sigh through the speaker box. "*You* know that, Daniel, and *I* know that," the agent said tiredly. "The secret to our keeping Courtney from zooming straight through the ozone layer is in making sure *she* doesn't know that. We only need one, to show to her. See what you can do, all right? We'll be in Chicago on Friday for a cable show. Have a new kit waiting for us when we arrive."

"I'll do that," Daniel answered, glad that Harry was being reasonable. "And tell Courtney I'd be happy to take her out to dinner when she gets back to New York."

The agent laughed, his deep chuckles filling the room. "Good idea. She's always had a soft spot for

you, hasn't she, Daniel? Even when you and Veronica—well, I gotta go now, to make nice-nice with the
talent. Ten percent is ten percent, right?''

Daniel broke the connection, then leaned back in his
high-backed leather swivel chair, the one he had in-
herited from Wilbur Langley when his father-in-law
retired from the company to divide his time between his
Park Avenue penthouse and his travels all over the
globe. Publishing was a crazy business, he reflected,
mentally composing a memo to the publicity department, but he loved it. He had always loved it.

Daniel had been at Langley since leaving college,
rapidly rising through the ranks by means of his mar-
ket-wise instincts and his uncanny ability to discover
average writers and mold them into bestselling authors. Now, at the age of thirty-four, he was at the peak
of his career. He was publisher of Langley Books, a
position he had been destined to occupy—even if he
hadn't been married to Wilbur Langley's only child,
Veronica.

Veronica. Harry's mention of his late wife's name
galled Daniel, for it seemed that even in New York,
where there was a scandal a minute, the gossip about
his failed marriage refused to fade away.

Thinking about Veronica naturally led Daniel to
thinking about their son, Richie. Wilbur Langley
hadn't been any more helpful with Richie than he had
with Veronica. Wilbur loved Richie, and meant well,
but he wasn't above using any method he could to earn
his grandson's favor. After a lifetime spent showering
his only daughter with lavish gifts and extravagant

indulgences, he seemed determined to repeat that destructive history with his only grandson.

"He ruined Veronica with his indulgences," Daniel said aloud, hitting his clenched fist against the desktop. "I'll be damned if I'll let him turn Richie into the same sort of spoiled, willful child!"

Joey was beginning to think the ice cream cone had been a mistake. The double-dipped mint chocolate chip ice cream was coolly delicious, but it was also melting a lot faster in the hot afternoon sun than she could eat it. Shifting the sugar cone from one hand to the other, she licked at her spread fingers, chasing a bright green rivulet of ice cream with her tongue as she stepped down from the curb and headed across Forty-second Street.

It was just past three o'clock, and she still had a little more than two hours to kill before she picked up Daniel Quinn for their return to Saucon Valley. She might as well walk down toward the Port Authority, to see if her friend Bo-Jo still kept his hot dog wagon on the same corner. Bo-Jo Hennessey was one of her favorite New York characters, and she had written about him in her manuscript. Wait until she told him she had an "in" at Langley Books! Besides, Bo-Jo would give her a soda and a clean napkin to wipe off her hands.

Suddenly, her tongue halting in mid-swipe, her light gray eyes widening in disbelief behind her sunglasses, Joey watched a young boy approaching her from the other curb. She blinked twice, doubting what she was seeing, but the vision refused to go away.

It was Richie Quinn, walking across Forty-second Street big as life, wearing a borderline-obscene graphic T-shirt and a pair of neon orange-and-electric-blue-striped shorts. His high-top sneakers barely clung to his sockless feet, the shoelaces undone and slapping against the street with every step he took. There was a huge army-green canvas knapsack strapped to his back and he was wearing a very smug, very self-satisfied grin. He even had a portable tape player strapped to his waist, the earphones stuck in his ears.

He looked totally at home on the busy streets of Manhattan.

"But he *belongs* in a three-story Colonial in safe, quiet Saucon Valley," Joey announced out loud, as if striving to convince herself that she wasn't really witnessing some sort of twisted mirage.

Richie didn't see her standing stock-still in the middle of the intersection, but just kept walking, absently looking to his left as an ambulance went racing by, its siren blaring. He was about to pass within inches of Joey when she reached out her free hand and took hold of his knapsack, hauling him back two paces.

"Park it right here, buster!" she ordered.

"Hey! You nuts or something? Let go! Knock it off!" Richie countered without turning around, struggling to free himself.

"When Michael Jackson sings opera, sweetcakes," Joey responded coldly. "All right, young man—explain yourself."

"*You!*" Richie exclaimed incredulously, turning his head to look straight into her eyes. His grimace was comically painful. "Of all the stupid, dumb luck! What do you think the odds are for something like this happening? A thousand to one? A million?"

"Oh, I don't know," Joey answered consideringly, eyeing her melting ice cream cone. "I've heard that if you stand on a New York street corner long enough, sooner or later you'll see everyone you've ever met."

The light changed and one of New York's "finest" approached the pair, pleasantly inquiring if they planned to abandon the middle of the intersection any time soon, or if he should just direct the traffic around them.

Joey smiled at the policeman, ignoring his lilting sarcasm, and politely begged his pardon, attempting to drag Richie back the way he had come, just as Richie tried to move in the other direction.

"She won't let go of me, officer," he told the policeman, his lower lip trembling in a way that immediately had Joey wishing spanking was still fashionable. "She must be some loony. I don't even know who she is. She just grabbed me and started telling me I remind her of her long-lost brother, or something. Don't arrest her or anything. She's harmless. I think she needs help, poor thing."

"Poor thing! Why, you *miserable*, fast-talking little beast, I'll—" Joey growled at the boy before looking up at the policeman, once more smiling brightly as that very tall, very large man stared down at her suspiciously, his fists on his hips. "Um, that is, please don't listen to him, officer," she pleaded quickly, suddenly feeling two feet high. "I work for his father. This boy is running away from home."

"Son?" the policeman questioned, looking at Richie intently.

Richie stood very straight, his arms at his sides, his chin in the air. "I never saw this woman before in my life!" he answered passionately, reminding Joey of every B-movie she had ever seen on the late-late show. She looked at him again, momentarily admiring the way he had somehow conjured up a tear in his left eye.

"Oh, good grief!" she declared, rolling her eyes. "Believe that one, officer, and I've got a great bridge you've just *got* to see. This is Richie Quinn, and his father is Daniel Quinn. Mr. Quinn works at Langley Books on Sixth Avenue. Like I said—I work for him."

"*As* I said—not *like* I said. You really should work on your grammar, you know," Richie corrected facetiously, too quietly for the policeman to overhear him. "She does not work for my father, or else I'd know who she is," he told the officer. "This is obviously a kidnap plot. I know all our employees. Why don't you ask her what she *says* she does for my father?"

"I'm his chauffeur!" Joey proudly announced at once, just before the officer's skeptical expression alerted her to the fact that she had charged headfirst into the neat little trap Richie had set for her.

She was dressed in a white blouse and black skirt—having left her vest and lace jabot in the limousine—and she was wearing orange-lensed sunglasses and bright purple high-top sneakers. Her hair was wind-blown, she looked young enough to be too young to buy a drink in Manhattan, and she was standing in the middle of the street with light green, chocolate-dotted goop dripping down her hand.

"Sure you are, honey," the policeman said soothingly, just as if she were a recent escapee from the home and apt to become dangerous at any moment, "and I'm the mayor of New York. Now, why don't you and the boy and I just walk on down to the station house on the corner, and I'm sure we can have this whole thing cleared up in no time."

"That's a great idea, sir," Richie complimented grandly, bowing as he backed toward the opposite curb. "But I don't think so. I have to go home now. My mother will be wondering where I am. Just let her go. I won't press charges. And I have your badge number, so my father will be sure to call your superiors to tell them how helpful you've been. Have a nice day, sir, and thank you."

Her upper arm gently but firmly held by the officer, Joey turned her head and watched as Richie Quinn tipped her a jaunty salute and melted into the crowd of pedestrians moving uptown. She yelled after him, "I'll get you for this, Richie Quinn! If it's the last thing I do, you rotten little monster, *I'll get you for this!*"

The policeman's indulgent grin disappeared like the sun behind a storm cloud. "Threats, is it now, missy? And to a nice young boy like that, worrying about his mother. For shame," he growled, his grip tightening on her upper arm. "Attempted kidnapping, and now terrorizing threats against that same child. All right, missy, we'll have it your way. Listen up. You have the right to remain silent—"

"What!" Joey turned to gape wide-eyed at the police officer as he read her her rights under the law. "You've got to be kidding, officer!" Out of the corner of her eye she saw Bo-Jo Hennessey standing beside his portable hot dog cart, practicing a tune on his harmonica. Immediately she shouted to him for help.

Bo-Jo, whom Joey had described in her manuscript as being "magnificently oblivious to the trials and tribulations of mere mortals" waved back at her and yelled, "Yo, Joey! Long time no see. How's the chauffeurin' business goin'?" before returning to his practice.

"...you have the right to have an attorney present during questioning—"

Joey knew when she was beaten. "Just great, Bo-Jo," she called out, grinning. "Couldn't be better. Catch you later." Under her breath she added, "In five to ten, I imagine, if I get time off for good behavior."

She was sitting on a worn wooden bench set against the far wall, slightly apart from the noise and confusion in the madhouse that made up the main receiving room of the police station. An elderly, poorly dressed man sat slumped beside her, snoring loudly, his head resting against her shoulder. Her feet were swinging back and forth a good four inches above the floor and she looked not so much angry as she did defeated. Defeated and frightened.

Daniel's heart went out to her. And he had thought walking the streets of New York would be boring. Obviously Joey Abbott had found a way around the problem. Richie had a lot to answer for this time.

He walked across the room, carefully threading his way between the startling array of felons and arresting officers until he was standing directly in front of his chauffeur. She looked so young, so appealing; he couldn't help himself. "So," he asked, tongue in cheek, "you come here often?"

Joey stiffened immediately, recognizing Daniel's voice. Her head went up with a snap, dislodging the grumbling, drunken man from her shoulder, and she glared at her boss. "Where is he?" she growled, gritting her teeth. "Where is that miniature mobster? You can have him when I'm done with him—but I get first dibs. I'm going to kill him—slowly, *very* slowly. And then I'm going to kill him all over again."

"You mean Richie, of course," Daniel answered reasonably, gently easing the still-sleeping man against the wooden arm of the bench and sitting down. "He's with his grandfather. I believe he made his anonymous phone tip to the police from there, and then the desk sergeant phoned me at my office. I've already called his grandfather and told him to have Richie ready to leave with us within the hour."

Joey gave a toss of her head, sniffing. She was still very angry. "And you think that makes it all better? Am I supposed to be grateful that he tried to clear my good name—considering the fact that he was the one who landed me in this mess in the first place? Maybe you think now I'll only want to kill him once instead of twice? That kid of yours should be kept on a strong leash, do you know that? At the very least he should come equipped with a warning label—like explosives."

Daniel stared at Joey, noted the high color in her cheeks, and felt his sense of humor tickled in spite of himself. "You're angry, aren't you? I have a sort of sixth sense about these things, you see," he said, silently deciding she looked pretty explosive herself.

"Angry?" Joey repeated, rising. "Don't be ridiculous. Why should I be angry? I've been hauled off to jail like a common criminal—and *fingerprinted*! Look at me, I'm all blue—and then locked in a holding pen with six of the most frightening-looking women this side of a horror show—one of them was named Peaches—and you wonder if I'm angry? No, I'm not angry—I'm homicidal!"

"Lower your voice, for crying out loud," Daniel advised quickly, standing up and looking around to make sure no one had overheard her. "That's how you got in here in the first place. Richie hadn't meant for you to be arrested. He was just frightened, and trying to get away from you. Everything would have worked out if you hadn't threatened him in front of the cop."

Joey put her hands on her hips and glared up at her employer. "You're kidding—right? I mean, you aren't actually *defending* that little monster! You can't be serious!"

And now she was supposed to go along to his grandfather's home and pick up the little darling to transport him back home? Fat chance! As far as Joey was concerned Daniel Quinn and his juvenile delinquent son could hitchhike back to Saucon Valley. She just wanted to forget this entire day had ever happened.

She started for the door, then stopped, her head drooping on her neck. "I forgot. I can't leave. Not until I pay the fine." She turned back to look at Daniel. "I don't suppose I could apply to you for a small loan? They don't seem to want to honor my credit cards."

Daniel was confused. He had arranged for all the charges to be dropped, promising to reprimand his son for his twisting of the truth, convincing the desk sergeant that the boy had meant no harm, that things had just somehow gotten out of hand. "What fine?" he asked, feeling more sorry for Joey by the moment.

Suddenly, after more than two hours of panic that had begun the moment the iron-barred door of the female holding cell closed behind her, the outright ridiculousness of the situation finally hit Joey, and she began to giggle. The giggles soon turned into hearty laughter, bringing tears to her eyes. *"Littering!"* she managed to squeak, holding on to herself as she rocked on her heels. "I got so mad at Richie that I threw my ice cream cone into the street in disgust. Officer O'Malley wrote me up for littering!"

Daniel was laughing along with her, for her laughter was infectious. "What flavor?" he managed to ask.

"Mint chocolate chip," Joey answered as they approached the desk sergeant and Daniel reached into his pocket to pull out his billfold. "My favorite."

"Adding insult to injury, I imagine?" Daniel commented as he waited for a receipt, then took hold of Joey's elbow and gently turned her toward the door. "If I buy you another cone, will you promise not to murder my son? He's no prize, but he's all I've got, and I'm rather attached to him. You understand, don't you?"

Joey took a deep breath of the warm late-afternoon air, feeling the tightness around her heart easing at last. How she had hated being locked inside that dreadful building, away from the light, her freedom gone. "Two scoops?" she asked, allowing Daniel's hand to remain on her elbow, secretly glorying in their slight physical contact.

"Two scoops," Daniel promised fervently as they descended the wide steps and headed for the cabstand on the corner, his smile very warm and very genuine.

A half hour later, after picking up Esmeralda at the parking garage, Daniel and Joey were on their way to Park Avenue and Wilbur Langley's penthouse apartment.

"I'll wait out here," Joey bit out from between clenched teeth, suddenly feeling rumpled and dirty and not up to meeting Wilbur Langley in his luxurious surroundings. She felt herself to be at enough of a disadvantage as it was, without opening herself up to Richie's sure-to-be-cutting remarks about her appearance. All she wanted now was to return to Saucon Valley as quickly as possible and then stand under a shower for at least an hour.

Daniel got out of the backseat and walked to the driver's door, pulling it open without ceremony. "You should keep that locked at all times," he cautioned automatically as he grabbed hold of her arm and half pulled her out onto the pavement. "Now, come with me. Richie's got some tall apologizing to do and I want to get it over with as soon as possible. I can't let him believe he's going to get away scot-free on this one or there'll be no dealing with him in the future."

Joey gave in, seeing that passersby were beginning to look at her. Normally this wouldn't bother her, but she had been the center of attention on one city street today and had learned her lesson. She went along quietly, following Daniel across the lobby to a private elevator he operated with a key he had taken from his billfold.

Thirty-seven floors of stony silence later, the silver metal doors whispered open and they stepped onto a snow-white cloud of carpeting that threatened to swallow Joey's ankles. The room they were in was more than large, it was immense, styled in stark black and white with touches of scarlet in the pillows, vases and a wall-sized painting, which was nothing more than a white background and an overwhelming pair of slightly parted, glistening red female lips. "How New York," Joey said noncommittally, hating the place on sight.

"Wilbur's in his starkly sexual period, or at least that's how he explained it to me," Daniel informed her tightly, and the censure in his voice made her look up at him. A muscle was working in his cheek as his gaze remained deliberately above the many marble statues of lovers embracing each other in a variety of casual to semishocking ways. "Rich!" he called out, obviously in a hurry to remove both his son and himself from the apartment as soon as possible. "Richie! Front and center—*now!*"

Suddenly, the deep plush of the carpet giving no warning of his entrance, a man appeared inside the room, obviously having been outside the windowed wall that opened onto a large balcony. "Daniel, my boy!" Wilbur Langley cried warmly, briskly walking across the expanse, his hand outstretched in greeting. "And this must be the loyal employee who got turned in to the coppers by my reprobate grandson. You rescued her, of course, just like the white knight you are. My, my, she looks quite the worse for wear, doesn't she?"

Joey looked at Wilbur Langley with mingled interest and anger. He was quite a man, tall, broad shouldered and extremely handsome despite his years. His silver mane topped a deeply tanned face, a face that wore a smile that seemed genuinely welcoming. "Mr. Langley," she responded wonderingly, knowing that she was in danger of succumbing to his smile in spite of herself. "Lovely place you've got here—if you're into 'weird.'"

Wilbur laughed out loud, taking her hand and raising it to his lips. "*Touché*, my dear," he congratulated. "I deserved that, didn't I? You don't like my decorations? I admit to being bored with them myself.

They were the result of the decorative talents of one of my recent companions, but it's time her inspirations followed her out of my life. Would you care to be in charge of the renovations? I've been thinking about blue—everything blue."

Joey couldn't fight it any longer. Wilbur Langley was a "character," and she'd always been intrigued by characters. "Blue would be nice—except denim blue. I don't think you could be comfortable in anything resembling a rustic setting. You seem more the midnight-blue-velvet type. What do you think, Daniel?"

The tic in Daniel's cheek was beating like a congo drum. "I think we'd better lasso Richie and get the hell out of here before Wilbur hires you away from me. Wilbur, where have you hidden him?"

The older man stepped back a pace, pressing a hand to his chest. "Hidden him, dear boy? *Moi?* As if I'd ever do such a thing. Whatever makes you think that?"

"Experience," Daniel retorted sharply, brushing past his father-in-law to walk toward the balcony. "Richie! Don't make this any harder than it has to be."

Richie Quinn stepped in front of the open doors, then moved inside the room to face his father. "Sorry, Dad. I didn't hear you the first two times you called me," he explained. Joey stifled a giggle, wondering if Richie realized exactly what he had said. He walked past his father, to stand beside Wilbur. "Miss Abbott," he went on, nodding slightly to Joey while deliberately avoiding her eyes. "Are you all right now? I'm sorry I couldn't stick around earlier, but you know how it is. I had already promised to meet Grandpa at the Plaza for high tea.''

''You *knew* he was coming to the city?'' Daniel asked his father-in-law. ''You knew, and you didn't phone me? Damn it, man—oh, what's the use in talking about it? You're worse than he is.''

Wilbur Langley hastened to smooth the ruffled waters and protect his grandson. ''I was going to tell you, Daniel. Right after high tea. The Plaza makes the best hot fudge sundaes in town, you know.''

''Oh, brother!'' Joey exclaimed, suddenly seeing the resemblance between Richie and his grandfather. No wonder Daniel was having so much trouble with his son. The two of them were, separately or together, a real piece of work. It was time she stepped in and fought her own battle with Richie, before her grievances got lost in the shuffle. She walked down the two steps into the living room, not stopping until she was nose to nose with the boy.

''Is there still a problem, Miss Abbott?'' Richie asked, his tone no longer so self-assured, for now both she and his father were looking at him strangely.

''*You*'ve got the problem, sonny boy,'' Joey shot back at him, lightly jabbing a finger against his chest. ''I'm not quite as civilized as your father and your grandfather, and I'm more than willing to make a scene. If you don't start apologizing to me in ten seconds—and apologizing hard—I'm going to start raining all over your little parade. You got that, buster?''

The three males in the room, all in various stages of shock, opened their mouths, but it was Richie who spoke. "I'm sorry, Joey. I didn't mean to get you into any trouble! Honest! I won't do it again." he promised, clearly amazed at the sound of his own voice, and just as clearly relieved that Wilbur's housekeeper took that moment to enter the room and announce dinner.

Chapter Four

Dessert? You've got to be kidding." Joey held out her hand and shook her head. "No, honestly, Wilbur, I couldn't swallow another bite. What? Mississippi Mud Pie? Oh, my *favorite*! It's like eating fudge in pastry. I give up—you've found my weak spot."

Wilbur deftly sliced a piece of the pie and handed the platinum-edged plate to Daniel, who grinned wickedly as he passed it to Joey. "We'll have to get more air in the tires before we head home," he teased, amazed that anyone so little could eat so much. He was liking his lady chauffeur more with each passing minute, and not just because she had succeeded so brilliantly in bringing Richie to heel. Richie's apology an hour earlier had been genuine and he'd been on his best behavior ever since.

"Do you know how much cholesterol there is in chocolate, Joey?" Richie teased now from across the glass-topped dining room table, rolling his eyes. "I can almost hear your arteries clogging."

Joey pointedly took a forkful of the pie and waved it lazily in Richie's direction before putting it into her mouth, her eyes slowly closing in ecstasy as the chocolate seduced her taste buds. "Ah, kiddo, but what a way to go!" she pointed out, sighing.

Richie's mouth worked silently as Joey slid a second piece of pie past her lips, her smile suggesting she had just died and gone to heaven.

Wilbur watched the exchange, measuring the thrusts and parries of the two combatants, then smiled as Richie quietly asked his grandfather to cut a slice of the pie for him. "Only a small one, please, Grandpa," he temporized. "After all, I did eat all my broccoli."

Daniel had also been watching Joey's play with the fork, and he felt a strange, hungry sensation growing in his belly that had nothing to do with Mississippi Mud Pie.

Joey Abbott intrigued him—there was no denying it. She was working in a profession he hadn't considered geared to female participation, yet she was one of the most feminine women he'd ever met. She might be small and perishable looking, but her character and determination seemed rock solid.

She'd handled the harrowing incident on the highway without turning a hair, when he had been sure they were moments away from death.

She'd dared to beard Richie in his protective grand-father's den and come off the rousing victor, capturing Wilbur Langley's admiration as well as Richie's, and Daniel's, respect.

But in those first few moments at the police station, when he had observed her unnoticed, he had seen a frightened, defeated Joey Abbott, a sad, caged canary who had lost the power to sing. He had been given a glimpse behind the lighthearted free spirit to the vulnerable woman beneath the cheerful exterior.

She was, he decided, a complex human being. She was also infinitely appealing.

The question was: what was he going to do about it, if anything? He had enough to deal with finding some way to reach Richie without entertaining thoughts of romancing his chauffeur. *Romancing his chauffeur?* Even the thought was ludicrous!

Wilbur rose at the head of the table, patting his flat stomach as if congratulating it on having received another fine meal. "Well, I guess you three will want to be on the road soon. Are you sure I can't interest you in an after-dinner brandy, Joey? Just a small one? You didn't even touch your wine. It's a long ride back to the wilds of Saucon Valley. Terrible place—I can't imagine life without the Met within strolling distance!"

"I'm driving, Wilbur, remember?" Joey answered, also rising. "I never drink when I'm on duty."

"Grandpa?" Richie interrupted, moving to Wilbur's side as they reentered the living room. "Do I really have to go with them? I just wanted to visit with you for a few days. I miss you so much."

Daniel, who had allowed himself to mellow a bit over dinner, felt his jaws tightening as his son began working his wiles on his grandfather. "Richie, we've been over this and over this," he broke in before Wilbur could respond. "You're never going to learn to live in Saucon Valley if you keep running back to New York every five minutes. You've got to give our new home a chance."

Give me a chance, Joey thought as she stood discreetly to one side, knowing that although Daniel hadn't said as much, it was what he had meant. She felt very sorry for Daniel Quinn. He might rule Langley Books, something she had found out during dinner, but when it came to his son he was totally at sea. It was sad to watch.

"Hey, wait a minute, guys," she broke in, reminding them of the promise she had exacted from Richie before Wilbur invited them to remain in town for dinner. "This kid has an appointment with me tomorrow, to sign up for baseball. That was the deal we struck before dinner, right?"

The look Richie threw her would have melted mint chocolate chip ice cream at ten paces, but Joey ignored it. She knew Richie was beginning to like her, in spite of himself. "You owe me, kiddo, remember? I'd accept your apology for having me tossed in the pokey if you'd promise to join my baseball team."

Richie pouted at her, trying one more time to wriggle out of his punishment, mostly out of habit. "You tricked me into it," he declared, then added brightly, "besides, the agreement would never stand up in court."

"Then aren't I the lucky one that this case will never see court," Joey observed mildly. "Your father okayed the arrangement, Richie, if you'll remember, and that's good enough for me."

Wilbur, who had admitted he thought Joey's idea of punishment was very amusing "in a droll sort of way" when first he'd heard it, seemed to undergo a change of heart. "Daniel," he said, facing his son-in-law, "don't you think Richie's been punished enough? After all, it was only a harmless prank. Not that Joey's wasn't a delightful suggestion, of course. I think we should all just forget it now."

"Oh, sure, that's easy for you to say. But then *you* didn't have to bunk with Peaches all afternoon," Joey groused, crossing her arms over her chest as Wilbur looked at her in confusion. "Besides, a deal's a deal. And you can turn off the waterworks, Richie—those tears won't cut any mustard with me. I've seen it all before, remember?"

Daniel looked from Richie to Joey, watching as the young woman outstared his son, and wondered why it bothered him that Joey seemed able to reach Richie while he could not. Granted, the two seemed to do nothing but argue, but Joey was winning those arguments, which was more than could be said for his own constant running battles with his son.

Besides, Richie was going to play baseball. Daniel had always wanted his son to play the game. Almost blackmailing him into joining a team wasn't Daniel's idea of the right way of going about the thing, but there were times when the end justified the means. "Richie," he warned in what he hoped was his most fatherly voice.

Richie shrugged his thin shoulders fatalistically. "All right, all right, I give up," he agreed, turning to kiss Wilbur goodbye. "But baseball's still stupid. I'm only going to do it for Joey."

Seeing the hurt that clouded Daniel's eyes, Joey winced, then hastened to bid her host good-night and hurried toward the elevator. Kids could be so darn cruel, she thought, sighing.

"I don't feel right about this, Joey. Are you sure you should be driving home alone on these country roads this late at night?"

Daniel was standing on the driveway, watching as Joey slipped into the backseat to retrieve the attaché case he had forgotten to take with him as he stepped out of the limousine. "Don't worry about me," he heard her say as he tried not to notice how shapely her exposed legs were as she leaned across the velvet seat. "It's only eleven o'clock. I don't turn back into a pumpkin for another hour." She backed out of the car and turned to hand him the case. "There you go, all set!"

Daniel reached out to take the case and their hands collided on the handle, each of them pulling back at the same time, as if they'd been stung. The case dropped to the driveway and Daniel bent to pick it up, giving him the time he needed to compose himself.

Joey used that same time to take a deep breath and give her head a small shake. She'd felt the electric current flowing between them in those few short seconds and it had startled her. Joey already knew she found Daniel attractive, but she hadn't counted on such a sharp, physical response at his slightest touch. She must be more desperate for male companionship than she had thought. She really should get out more.

"So," she heard him say as he straightened, "you'll be picking up Richie at three tomorrow afternoon? He'll be ready, if I have to handcuff him. That boy needs a lesson."

"That *boy* needs to be a boy," Joey replied quickly, speaking before she could think. "I—um, that is—I didn't mean—"

"Yes, you did," Daniel said, cutting her off. "And you're absolutely right. Half the time he acts old enough to be my father, and the rest of the time he behaves like a three-year-old. A particularly *backward* three-year-old. I'd like to apologize again for what he did to you today. I should ground him until he's thirty for hopping a bus to New York, but it was Wilbur who sent him the fare. How do I ground a man like Wilbur? He thinks he's Peter Pan—he'd just fly away."

Joey could see the pain in Daniel's eyes, and hear the confusion and sorrow in his voice even as he tried to make a joke. She hastened to assure him that she was none the worse for wear after her short stint in jail. "Hey, I already told you not to worry about it," she responded, deliberately smiling. "Not every girl can brag about being fingerprinted. I just hope I look all right on my mug shot.''

"We never did get you another mint chocolate chip ice cream cone," Daniel pointed out, knowing he was keeping her talking just so that he wouldn't have to say good-night and go inside the house. Richie was in the house, waiting to pounce, after sitting silent as a stone beside him in the backseat all the way home. He was sure of it. He also was sure he wasn't up to another confrontation before midnight.

"That's all right, really," Joey told him, suddenly feeling extremely protective of this very large, very self-sufficient male. She wished she could say something that would take that haunted, hurt look from his face. "I'll let you owe me. Well, I guess I should be on my way. Tell Richie to be ready by two-thirty. I want to have time to introduce him to the other kids before practice starts." She turned to leave, then another thought struck her. "He has a glove, doesn't he?"

"Damn!"

"I'll take that as a no," she said, turning to face Daniel once more. "There's a good sporting goods store near the park if you want me to take him there before practice. An outfielder's glove, I imagine, as I have a feeling Richie is a natural-born right fielder.''

"That's where we always put the kids who couldn't catch a Ping-Pong ball in a barrel," Daniel remembered, scowling as he spoke. He'd played first base himself, both in high school and college. The thought of having his son, his only hope of immortality, shipped off to right field was very lowering. "Does it have to be right field?"

Joey shrugged. "It's a start," she offered lamely, then turned on her heels once more, wishing she had never started all of this in the first place. She should have sentenced Richie to washing Esmeralda twice a week for a month. She hadn't meant to cause Daniel any more pain than he already had. She wouldn't want to fight a tug-of-war over a child of hers against Wilbur Langley.

"A hundred dollars enough?" he called after her.

"A hundred dollars? Enough for what?" Joey's mind grasped at understanding Daniel's words.

"For a mitt," he explained. "It's been a while since I priced one. I want him to have a good one—oversize, to give him every chance at snagging a fly ball."

Joey shook her head. "For a hundred dollars I can get him a mitt *and* a butterfly net—for the really hard-to-catch balls, you understand."

Daniel blushed and was thankful that Joey couldn't see his painfully flushed cheeks in the dim light radiating from the porch. "Whatever," he said, looking after her as she walked around Esmeralda to get back behind the wheel. She was leaving, and he didn't want her to go—and not just because he wanted to delay his talk with Richie. "Don't forget to lock your door."

"Good night, Daniel. See you Friday."

She had already turned the key in the ignition when Daniel's knuckles tapped at the tinted window, and she lowered it warily, wondering what was wrong.

"What would you say," he began, bending down to lean in the opening, "if I tagged along with you and Rich tomorrow? I mean, I had planned to work at home tomorrow, so it isn't as if I'd be losing time I couldn't make up somewhere else in the day. That is, if you don't think I'd get in the way or anything..."

Now it was Joey's turn to rescue Daniel. "I think that would be just fine," she told him hurriedly before he could feel foolish for begging to share some time with his own son. "We'll see you at two o'clock—so we can stop at the sporting goods store."

"We?"

Joey laughed, then explained. "We, Daniel. As in Esmeralda and me." She patted the steering wheel. "*This* is Esmeralda. We go everywhere together."

As Daniel watched the gleaming white limousine pull out of the driveway onto the narrow macadam road he scratched his head, wondering how Richie was going to take this latest development, then realizing he didn't care if Richie liked it. *He* liked it very much.

In the end, Joey left Esmeralda at home, opting instead to pick up Daniel and Richie in her five-year-old baby-blue Mercedes convertible, even if that meant she wouldn't be able to take the entire team to the local ice cream shop for a treat after practice.

Esmeralda was too formal for what she wanted to accomplish, for the mood she wanted to set. After all, how could she expect the other kids to take Richie seriously if he arrived in a limousine, with his chauffeur opening the door for him as he stepped out onto the baseball diamond with his brand-new, unbroken-in outfielder's glove? It would be the kiss of death!

Of course, there was another reason for leaving Esmeralda behind in the garage, and that other reason was Daniel Quinn. Joey rather liked the idea of having Daniel riding up front in the passenger seat beside her as they drove to the field. She wanted to know this man better, whether it was professionally correct to do so or not.

Daniel stepped out of the front door of the rambling brick Colonial as Joey pulled into the driveway, and she nearly ran the Mercedes into a rhododendron bush when she saw how he was dressed. Gone was the dark pin-striped suit and sedate tie, and with it the air of a successful businessman. In its place were a broad-shoulder-hugging, kelly-green polo shirt and white cotton duck slacks that accentuated his narrow waist and long, muscular legs. The front of his chestnut hair lifted slightly in the breeze and he was wearing a smile that seemed relaxed, almost boyish.

This man could make a serious dent in my heart, Joey decided, turning off the ignition and stepping out onto the driveway, purposely keeping the Mercedes between her and her very appealing contract client. ''Hi,'' she breathed, unsurprised to find that this single mundane word was suddenly the limit of her vocabulary.

''Hi, yourself,'' Daniel countered, his white-toothed grin forcing her to clutch the side-view mirror to maintain her footing. What had happened since she picked Daniel up yesterday morning to change her

acknowledgment of his attractiveness into a wild, un-
controllable crush?

"Rich will be out in a minute."

Mention of Richie's name effectively wiped the inane smile from Joey's face as reality came crashing
back in on her. Richie. The reason for their meeting
today. The ten-year-old walking emotional accident,
looking for a place to happen. "Is that a promise," she
asked, tilting her head to one side, "or just wishful
thinking?"

Daniel's expression turned stern. "It's a promise,"
he said, walking over to lay a hand on the hood of the
Mercedes. "Don't look now, but Esmeralda seems to
have shrunk—and turned blue. Not that it matters. We
won't be needing this today, if you don't mind. We'll
take my car, if you just point me in the right direction."

Like many good drivers, Joey hated being relegated
to the passenger side of the front seat. If her brother,
Andy, had been there he would have given an exagger-
ated grimace and covered his head with his hands the
moment Daniel spoke. But Andy wasn't there, and
Joey didn't explode or make the suggestion that Daniel was being slightly chauvinistic. She just reached inside the car, pocketed the keys and said, "Fine by me,
Daniel," her expectations for their day together soar-
ing higher and higher.

The sound of the front door of the house slamming
closed made them both turn their heads in that direction just in time to see the door open once more and the
red-faced Mrs. Hemmings emerge behind Richie, a

large wooden spoon in her hand. "I don't care who your grandfather is, young man, you'd better not sass me again, not if you know what's good for you!"

"Oh, yeah," Richie countered, hands on hips, "well, we'll just see about that, won't we? Grandpa says you're just the hired help, and the hired help don't tell the employer what to do. Grandpa says—"

"Richie!" The single word shot through the air like a booming cannonball slamming against a brick wall. Joey winced as Daniel started back up the steps to the covered porch, fire in his eyes. "Apologize to Mrs. Hemmings at once!"

"Dad," Richie remarked, surprised. "I didn't see you out here."

"Obviously. Now, what's going on here?"

Both housekeeper and son began speaking at once, so that Joey only heard the random words "farina" and "make my own bed" and "I've never seen the like before" as Daniel looked from one to the other, his frown deepening into a furious scowl.

So much for romance. Joey let an exasperated sigh escape her lips, then leaned back against the Mercedes to watch the action. Daniel surprised her. She had decided that he was a loving father, but totally inept at handling his son—and maybe even a little afraid of him. If he had been any or all of these things, he was certainly a fast learner at finding ways to correct his previous shortcomings.

"Let me get this straight," Joey heard him say when the complaints finally stopped. "Richie—you don't make up your own bed in the morning? Saunders never said anything—Saunders was our housekeeper in New York, Mrs. Hemmings," he told the woman. "You're nearly eleven, Richie. Beginning tomorrow, you'll make your own bed or sleep in it unmade. Now, what's this about farina?"

"He refuses to eat it, that's what," Mrs. Hemmings said, shaking her head. "My Herbert ate farina every morning of his life, and he still would if he wasn't dead."

"It's probably what killed him," Richie sniped, sticking out his chin, and Joey found herself hiding a smile behind her hand.

"There—he said it again, Mr. Quinn!" Mrs. Hemmings pointed out, waving the spoon in Richie's direction. "In all my born days, I can't remember a child with such an evil tongue. I saw this movie last night—"

"The Bad Seed?" Daniel interposed wryly, believing he knew what the housekeeper was trying to say.

Mrs. Hemmings shook her head. *"Mary Poppins,"* she corrected. "The one with Julie Andrews in it. Such a pretty girl—and what a lovely voice! Anyway, I have to tell you, Mr. Quinn, I'm no Mary Poppins. She might have been able to handle this boy of yours, but not me! I think I'll have to hand in my notice."

Richie's eyes lit with triumph. Joey saw it, standing twenty feet away. Daniel was closer. He not only saw it—he reacted. "Richie," he said, his tone the one he must normally have reserved for the boardroom, for Joey hadn't heard it before, even in those tense moments in Wilbur's penthouse, "you are to *apologize* at

once to Mrs. Hemmings. Furthermore, beginning today you are going to be assigned daily chores in order
to *help* Mrs. Hemmings. We'll start with making your
own bed, taking out the trash and . . . and . . ."

"And clearing the table after meals," Mrs. Hemmings added helpfully, the light that had suddenly died
in Richie's eyes now gleefully gleaming in hers.

Joey had to turn away to hide another smile as Richie, once more caught off stride, quietly apologized
to the housekeeper before both he and his father left
the porch and approached the Mercedes.

"All set?" Daniel asked with a forced smile as he
opened the passenger door, forgetting that he had
planned to drive his own car. Clearly he was more upset by this latest knowledge about his son than he was
willing to reveal to Joey. "Richie," he ordered, "get
yourself into the backseat, and keep your mouth shut."

"Hi, Richie," Joey said cheerfully, receiving an un-
intelligible mutter from the boy in reply. Pulling the car
keys from her pocket, she slid behind the wheel and
turned the ignition, glad she had opted to put the top
down, for the heat emanating from the backseat would
have made a closed car feel like an inferno. "First stop,
Crazy Louie's discount sporting goods store," she announced, mentally crossing her fingers in the hope the
remainder of the afternoon would go smoothly.

"Tuesday, Thursday and Saturday? That's great! I
go in to the city Monday, Wednesday and Friday. It
couldn't be better. You can count me in!"

Joey overheard Daniel's answer to head coach Steve Mitchum's suggestion that he sign on as the team's first base coach. Her heart did a small flip in her chest as she lifted her eyes to the blue summer sky and whispered a fervent "thank you."

It had been, all things considered, a most wonderful afternoon. For Daniel. Clearly he was in his element on a ball field, shagging balls in the outfield, taking charge of batting practice for a while and even helping instruct the pint-size pitching staff.

He looked years younger than Steve, and much more physically fit, even though both men were about the same age. His chestnut hair tamped down beneath a blue Bulldogs baseball cap, he had even taken a few swings of his own during batting practice, knocking three balls over the center field fence. Running around the bases after the last hit, he laughingly doffed his cap as the team cheered him on, and then, sliding into home plate, he completely ruined his white slacks.

As she sat in the shade beside the cement dugout, Joey allowed her smile to fade as she caught sight of Richie—standing among the ankle-high white-topped dandelions in right field. Obviously this first practice wasn't going as swimmingly for the ten-year-old Quinn.

"There's going to be many a splinter in that boy's bottom before the end of the season if we can't find some way to reach him," she mused, shaking her head as she remembered how painfully inept Richie looked at bat, on the bases and now deep in no-man's-land.

And Richie was hating every minute of it, Joey was sure. She had seen him looking at his father, his expression confused, as that man had patiently helped another child adjust his grip on the bat. Richie's pain had nearly broken her heart. Richie loved his father, just as Daniel loved his son. But getting them both to admit to that love was going to be a problem.

Steve had taken charge of Richie at the beginning of the practice, just as Joey had hoped, but he had admitted to her only a few minutes earlier that the boy did not exactly show signs of being a natural athlete. From her vantage point beside the dugout, Joey had watched Daniel watching Richie, and it was obvious to her that Daniel's opinion coincided with Steve's.

"There has to be something I can do," she declared, her gray eyes narrowed as she rose to her feet, brushing off the seat of her jeans.

"Do about what?" Daniel asked, coming up beside her. Without waiting for her answer, he continued. "This is great, isn't it? You know Steve asked me to help coach the team, don't you? You don't mind, do you? I mean, I'm not stepping on any toes, am I?"

Oh, brother, Joey thought, sighing. *I thought a man had to be older than Daniel is before he entered his second childhood.* "No, I don't mind," she told him honestly as they walked across the first-base line toward the pitching mound. "Steve needs more help, as I can only be here when I'm not on the road with Esmeralda. But I don't know how Richie is going to take your good news. He doesn't seem exactly thrilled to be here, does he?"

Daniel turned his head to look toward right field. Richie was sitting on the grass, his new fielder's glove stuck on his head to shade his eyes from the late-afternoon sun. "He looks lost, doesn't he?" he commented, sighing. "Poor kid. I would have gone to him, but Steve said dads shouldn't coach their own kids. He told me experience has taught him that we tend to be too hard on our own flesh and blood. How could I be hard on Richie? I could cry for him. He looks like a fish out of water."

Joey knew Daniel was reaching out to her, asking for her help, and she stubbornly ignored any niggling thoughts that she could be getting in over her head. She sought wildly in her mind, then heard herself saying, "We've tried him everywhere except on the pitching mound. Do you think we should give him a try?"

The practice had wound down and Steve and most of the team had already gone. Daniel looked around for a moment, then shrugged. "Why not? It's worth a shot. Hey, Richie! Come here a minute."

Richie got up slowly, then jogged in to join them on the pitcher's mound. "I hope you're satisfied," he accused coldly, looking directly at Joey, his expression more hurt than angry. "I looked like a real jerk out there. Everybody was laughing at me."

Joey ignored him, even as she pitied him. "Your dad and I want to see if you can pitch," she told him, already walking back to the dugout to get a catcher's mask and mitt. "Daniel," she called back over her shoulder, "you can toss a few in to me to give him the general idea."

"She's kidding, right?" Richie asked his father, pulling a face. "I mean, she really doesn't think I'm going to do this, does she? Dad, help! Get me out of here.''

"She's Joey to you, or Ms. Abbott," Daniel answered, slipping his own glove onto his right hand, watching appreciatively as Joey, in jeans and halter top, walked away from them. "And no, she's not kidding. Now, pay attention. We're both left-handed, so you can just imitate my moves."

Richie spread his feet and lifted his chin in defiance. He'd had a long afternoon, and clearly he felt he had been pushed as far as he was willing to go. He had begun to like Joey, and now he felt she had betrayed him. "I won't do it, and you can't make me. I know what you're doing. You don't really care about me. If you want to ask Joey out, go ask her. I don't want her anyway!"

"That's enough! Go to the car—*now*!" The sound of Daniel's voice raised in anger had Joey looking quickly toward the pitching mound, just in time to see Richie blindly running toward the Mercedes.

She turned to go to the boy, then looked at Daniel and realized that for the moment, he needed her more. He was still standing on the pitching mound, staring at his raised left hand as if it didn't belong to him. She ran to his side, taking his arm. "Daniel," she asked softly, "what is it? What happened?"

He looked down at her, visibly shaken, his blue eyes bleak. "I raised my hand to him," he said, speaking as if he were slightly dazed. "I almost slapped my son. I've never laid a finger on him, Joey—*ever*—but just now..." He pressed a hand to his eyes. "I had such high hopes for today. I thought he liked you. I thought we could begin to establish a relationship, find some sort of common ground. What a joke! My God, what am I going to do now? Maybe Wilbur's right, and I should let Richie go live with him.''

Joey bit her lip, trying not to succumb to the need to slide her arms around Daniel and lend him her comfort. "You'd do that?" she asked, squeezing his forearm, her voice deliberately mocking. "He's your son, Daniel, not a throwaway soda bottle. You have to make this work, for your sake as well as his."

Daniel placed his free hand over hers on his arm. He smiled, but his smile was wan, defeated. "A throwaway soda bottle, Joey? That's an unusual comparison. You're right, however. I've got to go on trying. Richie's been through a lot, you know."

Joey nodded, not really wanting to hear more. She was getting too involved as it was. "Growing up without a mother isn't easy. I know that from my own experience," she offered sympathetically. "But you're a good father, and you and Richie will eventually work things out."

"Eventually," Daniel repeated dourly. "I don't know if I can wait that long."

Joey shrugged, then bent to pick up their gloves and started back to the dugout to gather up the rest of their gear, Daniel tagging along beside her like a stray puppy intent on following her home. How did she always manage to get herself mixed up in everyone else's problems? "We'd better not leave Richie alone too long, Daniel. If that kid of yours is half as smart as I give him credit for, he'll soon get bored waiting for us, hot-wire my car and head for the New Jersey Turn-pike.''

Daniel nodded, taking the heavy canvas bag full of bats and mitts from her and hefting it onto his shoul-der as they walked to the car. "Much as I'm sure you've seen enough of anybody named Quinn to last you a lifetime, Joey, would you go to dinner with me tonight? I'd really like to talk with you some more.''

Joey looked up at him. "About Richie, I sup-pose?'' she asked, feeling her heart sink to her toes.

"About Richie,'' Daniel admitted, then added softly, "and... other things.''

The "other things'' had her heart making a spectac-ular rebound, repositioning itself somewhere high in her throat. Consigning her feelings of personal pro-tection to a far corner of her mind, Joey smiled up at him, saying, "I hear they make a great version of Mississippi Mud Pie at some new restaurant on Cedar Crest Boulevard. I can't be bought, Daniel—but that doesn't mean I'm not open to bribes.''

Chapter Five

The restaurant had been decorated in an upscale, metropolitan decor that blended well with the more personal, homey atmosphere created by the staff. Joey and Daniel had spent more than a half hour sipping their drinks while waiting for their table to open, speaking of generalities and enjoying the people around them.

It was only after they had placed their orders that Daniel took a deep breath and searched his mind for some way to begin explaining the complex bundle of nerves that was his son. It wasn't going to be easy for him, and the sight of Joey sitting across the small round table from him wasn't helping matters at all.

He had known she was pretty, and had already privately acknowledged that he was physically attracted to her. But he'd had no idea of the shattering effect a simple, sophisticated, slim black sheath, a small amount of artfully applied makeup and the soft candlelight flickering against her smooth skin would have on his powers of concentration.

She was sitting quietly, a miniature oasis of calm in his increasingly frenetic world, interestedly observing her surroundings, her moist red lips parted in a slight smile as her intelligent gray eyes sparkled with delight. Was her delight with the evening, or with him? And why did it matter so much to him?

He realized that they had been sitting in silence for almost five minutes. "About Richie—" he began after clearing his throat.

Joey turned her head to face him and she leaned forward slightly, as if encouraging him to confide in her. "You may not believe this, Daniel, but I really do like your son. He may be a handful, but you have to admit—he's never boring."

Daniel averted his eyes and began idly toying with his salad fork. "He's a pretty likable kid. You're probably wondering why I lost my temper with him this afternoon."

Joey smiled, shaking her head. "Actually, using my own brief experience with him as a guide, I'm wondering what took you so long. Surely you must have been tempted long before today."

They both laughed, easing the sudden tension that had sprung up between them with just the mention of Richie's name. Daniel wasn't thrilled that Joey recognized that his son was a problem, but it was a relief to finally have someone agree with him. Richie's teachers in the private school he attended in Manhattan had had nothing but praise for his outstanding academic achievements, and the doting Wilbur Langley refused to listen to a single word against his grandson, believing the child to be perfect in every way.

"My wife, Veronica, died when Richie was three," Daniel began quietly, knowing no other way to start than at the beginning. "After her death, and with Wilbur retiring from the company shortly after the funeral to travel the world, I devoted myself almost exclusively to Langley Books, even more than I had before she died. Richie is now making me pay the price of my neglect of him."

Joey raised her eyebrows skeptically. "I'd hardly term Richie a neglected child."

Daniel shook his head. "Materially, no, he's not. Wilbur showered him with gifts from abroad for years, then doubled his efforts when he returned to New York three years ago and found that his grandson was now old enough to be a companion of sorts. Richie had always been a quiet child, you understand, so it was easy for me to turn most of his care over to Saunders, and the nurse I hired when he was still a baby. It wasn't until Wilbur reentered our lives that the real trouble started, although I should have been paying more attention to the warning signs."

"Warning signs?" Joey prompted when Daniel fell silent.

He nodded. "Richie knew the alphabet and numbers when he was two, and it was all uphill from there.

By the time he was seven I didn't have a clock or radio in the whole apartment that he hadn't taken apart and put back together three times. I enrolled him in gifted classes at the recommendation of his teachers, then left the raising of him to others while I buried myself in my own work." He leaned forward, lowering his voice. "You know, I read somewhere that many gifted children may be able to run rings around other people intellectually, yet not possess the common sense to come in out of the rain."

Joey laughed out loud. "Daniel! You're overreacting. Richie has plenty of common sense. I'm sure he'd at least take an umbrella."

"Really?" Daniel leaned back once more. "Did my son display any common sense when he hopped a bus to New York? Have you ever been inside the Port Authority? He's only ten years old. Anything could have happened to him!"

Joey took a sip of her wine. "You have a point there. But it was Wilbur's idea, wasn't it? You can't blame a ten-year-old for listening to his grandfather."

"All roads lead back to Wilbur Langley," Daniel said, sighing. "You know," he told her, his voice filled with yearning, "all I ever wanted was a kid I could play ball with—but somehow, we both seem to have gotten lost along the way."

Joey felt sorry for Daniel, yet was angry with him for kicking himself so hard. "You can't blame yourself for what you think are your failures with Richie. It must have been hard for you—for both of you—when your wife died. It was only natural for you to bury yourself in your work.''

Daniel's voice hardened. ''Veronica walked out on us when Richie was six months old. He never really knew her, except for the few times she descended out of nowhere to shower gifts on him before flitting off somewhere else. Our marriage had been a mistake from the beginning, and I was just as glad to see her go running off in search of what she called fun. I was sorry she had to die in that plane crash, but I'd be a hypocrite if I said I had still loved her.''

Joey sat back while the waiter placed two tossed salads on the table, her expression turning pensive. ''I don't know what to say, Daniel. 'I'm sorry' just doesn't seem to cover it. But you have Richie with you now, away from Wilbur and his influence—which I assumed prompted you to move to Saucon Valley in the first place. You'll just have to take it one day at a time. Your relationship will grow, if you both give it a chance.''

''Yes,'' Daniel agreed, giving her the ghost of a smile. ''But now there's another complication.''

''Another—I don't understand.''

Daniel reached across the table and took her hand. ''You, Joey. You're the new complication.''

''*Me?* What do I have to do with anything?''

''Richie likes you,'' Daniel explained, ignoring his salad. ''I don't think he wanted to, but he does just the same. He wants your approval, which is why I found him in the garage tonight, tossing a baseball against a target he'd painted on the wall. You've reached him, Joey—when I couldn't.''

Joey was pleased, but confused. "I'm flattered. But then why did he run away this afternoon, instead of letting us watch him pitch?''

Daniel took a deep breath, then explained. "He doesn't know which Quinn you want for a friend. It's either/or in Richie's mind.''

"He doesn't think I'm only pretending to like him in order to get to you, does he?'' she asked once the waiter had removed the uneaten appetizers and replaced them with the entrées. *Stupid question, Joey,* she told herself. *Nothing like admitting you find the guy attractive.*

Daniel shook his head at her mistaken impression, hastening into speech. "On the contrary. This afternoon, just before I sent him to the car, Richie accused *me* of using him to get to *you!*"

"Oh." Joey's voice had grown very small. So had she, Daniel observed in private amusement, as she leaned against the high-backed chair, as if drawing herself into a protective shell. Daniel's pulse sped up, believing he had frightened her, but a moment later she recovered her composure and sat forward once more. She propped her elbows on the table, laid her chin in her hands and inquired sweetly: "So, was your own personal *Wunderkind* right, Mr. Quinn? *Are* you trying to 'get to' me?''

Daniel's head snapped back slightly. He had expected questions from Joey, but he hadn't expected her to be quite so direct. "I don't know," he answered truthfully. "Strangers don't exactly come up to you to shove a paper bag over your head, do they? I mean, you are very attractive. I'd have to be blind not to see that."

Joey chewed on a bite of steak, her brow furrowed in thought. "I've decided to take that as a compliment," she told him a moment later. "I'm sure there was one hidden in there somewhere."

Daniel laughed aloud, feeling the tension that had knotted his shoulders draining away, leaving him feeling lighter, and almost carefree. "You're something else, Joey Abbott," he said, reaching across the table to take her hand in his and squeeze it gently. "You remind me of a fresh spring breeze after a long, cold winter. I don't think I can remember the last time I laughed out loud."

"Poor boy," Joey teased, although he could see that his words had touched her. "But I think you made a good choice, moving to Saucon Valley. This is a family-oriented kind of place, a place where you and your son can really come to know each other. Richie will think so too, once he understands that this move is permanent and takes that chip off his shoulder."

"He still hates baseball, even if he's willing to try, just to gain your approval," Daniel pointed out, in case either of them was beginning to feel too confident. "He hates the sport, the boys on the team and the coaches—all of us. Richie has become an equal-opportunity hater."

Joey's chin came up. "I wasn't expecting a miracle today, Daniel. Give him time, he'll come around. And if he can't cut it as a player, we can introduce him to the wonderful world of statistics. Richie seems to be attracted to numbers. There are records kept for everything a player does—except for the most sneezes while at bat in a doubleheader, and there will probably be one for that any day now.''

Shaking his head in wonderment at her persistence, as well as her thoughtfulness, Daniel considered her latest idea. ''He could enter all the players' statistics into his computer,'' he mused. ''The kids would be all over him, wanting to know their batting averages. Joey, I think you just might have hit on the perfect solution!''

''Good,'' Joey replied, ''although I still don't believe Richie was throwing that ball tonight just to please me. I saw how he was looking at you today while you coached those other boys. Richie loves you, Daniel, never doubt that. Now, let's eat. I have to clean my plate so you'll reward me with a slice of that wonderful pie that got me here in the first place.''

''Exactly how much land do you and your brother own, Joey?'' Daniel was standing in the middle of the wide gravel driveway, trying with narrowed eyes to pierce the darkness beyond the well-lit barn that served as Esmeralda's garage. ''I noticed when I picked you up earlier that you're rather isolated out here. Was this once a working farm? I remember seeing several smaller buildings besides the house and barn.''

''Andy and I only own thirty-five acres now, much less than when we actually farmed for a living.'' Joey was leaning against the side of Daniel's Cadillac, randomly thinking that he looked quite at home in this setting. "Dad sold some acreage right after we bought the place, in order to make improvements on the house and outbuildings—little conveniences, like indoor plumbing—and I sold more to take care of Andy's college expenses after Dad died. But that's the end of it—the rest is ours, no matter how much we're offered for it."

"You've been approached, of course. You're too close to the new highway not to have been." Daniel knew what he had paid for his building lot, and was curious to learn why Joey and her brother had turned down what could only be an enormous profit.

Joey didn't really hear him. She was thinking about the loan manager's advice that she put up part of the farm as collateral for her purchase of a second limousine. The thought still rankled. She'd turned him down flat, of course. No matter how sure she was that Abbott Aristocrat Limousines would be successful, there was no way she was going to put Andy's and her inheritance—their last visible link to their father—on the line. No way.

"Joey?" Daniel leaned against the car next to her, trying to get her attention.

"My dad was an engineer," she began softly, as if speaking to herself. "Not as in a choo-choo, railroad engineer, but an electrical engineer, and a darn good one. He was so good that he was rarely ever home. He was always working, always on call. Andy and I used to call him Uncle Daddy, because we saw him so seldom. Then one day, about a month after our mother died, Dad walked away from his career and put everything he had into this farm.'' She tilted her head and smiled up into Daniel's eyes. ''We didn't have to call him Uncle Daddy anymore. He gave us more than this farm—he gave us himself. Every day of his life, until he died.''

Joey's face was luminous with love as she spoke of her father. ''Your father must have been a wonderful, caring, unselfish man,'' Daniel said, sliding an arm around her shoulders and pulling her to his side as they both leaned against the Cadillac. She fit against him perfectly, the top of her head nestling against his chest. ''Now I understand why you and your brother turned out so well.''

''Thank you,'' Joey responded, humbled, and a little sad. ''Dad was quite a teacher.''

''Joey, I—'' Daniel began, pushing himself away from the Cadillac to stand in front of her, his hands on her shoulders.

''Yes, Daniel?'' Joey prompted helpfully. She was looking up at him, her gray eyes misty with memories he couldn't share.

''Oh, the hell with it.'' He groaned, lowering his head. ''I can't fight it anymore.'' His lips covered hers, his arms closing more fully around her as her hands slid up his chest to lock behind his neck, wordlessly showing him that he hadn't been wrong to believe she'd accept his touch.

Her mouth was warm and soft beneath his and after a moment he dared to deepen the kiss, astonished at the sudden yearning to possess her that raced through his body. She was so small, yet so strong, so worldly-wise, yet so vulnerable. He felt fiercely protective of her even as his mind raced to find a way to breach all her defenses.

And she was so willing, so giving. He sensed that she trusted him to be gentle with her, to take only what she was willing to give and not press for more. He could feel her trembling beneath his hands as they stood alone in the dark, the sounds of the summer night their only companions, their only censors. Her trust in him brought him back to his senses even as his body cursed him for a fool.

"Oh, Joey," he breathed huskily at last, breaking their kiss to press her head against his chest. "You don't know how lucky you are. That was some first kiss."

"Yes, I do, and yes, it certainly was," she responded shakily, as breathless as he. "As a matter of fact, on a scale of one to ten, I'd rank it a twenty-three."

She could feel his chest move as he chuckled, easing the tension between them that had been growing ever since dinner. "You know," he said, rubbing the side of her head with his hand, mussing her hair with his big fingers, "I've never kissed a chauffeur before. It's quite an experience."

"I can imagine," Joey responded with a laugh, moving away from him slightly, so that she could take his hand and begin walking toward the house. "I've never kissed a client before, if it comes down to that. You do know that, don't you?"

Daniel stopped walking to pull her in front of him and lift her chin with his finger as they stood within the soft yellow glow of the porch light. "I do know that, Joey," he said softly, bending to kiss the tip of her nose. "And I won't kiss you like that again—at least not tonight—so you don't have to go running for cover. That's what you're so tactfully trying to do, isn't it?"

Joey looked up at him, wiggling her eyebrows comically. "Not too subtle, huh?" she asked. "Sorry about that. I guess I was being a bit childish."

He led her toward the old-fashioned porch swing and they sat down, still holding hands. "You were being a bit intelligent, and I don't blame you," he admitted wryly. "But that doesn't mean I'm ready to go home. It's barely midnight. Tell me more about your father."

Joey was more than eager to comply with his request, for she, too, was reluctant to end the evening. "All right," she agreed, "what do you want to know?"

Pulling her against his chest once more, only because it felt so right to have her there, Daniel said, "Oh, I don't know. Just let your mind roam free, and tell me whatever occurs to you."

Joey looked up at the quarter moon and smiled as a memory took hold of her. "'Look at that glass of milk, Joey,' Dad used to tell me," she began slowly. "'To some people,' he'd say, 'it's half-empty. You know what it is to me? It's half-full. You know how the weatherman says it's partly cloudy? He's wrong, pumpkin. It's partly sunny. It's the same with everything in life. It's all in the way you look at it. Always remember that.'"

"That's a good philosophy," Daniel told her, beginning to understand Joey's optimistic outlook.

"Yes," Joey answered, her voice suddenly sad. "Yes, it is. It's also all too easy to forget. Unfortunately, I forgot it myself for a while. After Dad died I threw myself into my studies at college, commuting so that I could take care of Andy. After I graduated I was offered a job with Ransom Computers and I jumped at it, to help with Andy's tuition. I wanted to keep busy, busy to the point where I didn't have either the time or the energy to miss Dad, the man who had meant the world to me. I really believed I would be happier that way."

"I can understand that," Daniel told her. "When Veronica left I buried myself in work, and after she died I did everything but live at the office. If you work hard enough, you don't have any time to think. It wasn't until I realized that I was losing Richie that I woke up to what I was doing, what I was missing."

Joey pushed at the porch floor with her toes, setting the swing into motion. "You were lucky to have Richie," she told him. "I had Andy, but he was older, more independent, and by the time he was a senior in high school I was so involved with climbing the corporate ladder that he was pretty much on his own. After he went off to college I worked even harder, to avoid coming home to an empty house. Besides, the money was good. No, let me amend that. The money was great."

"Let's all hear it for greed," Daniel slid in, laughing at her dogged honesty.

"It sure does make the world go round, doesn't it?" Joey remarked, not looking for an answer, but lost in her own memories. "But it only works so long. Then, some rainy morning, as you sit slumped behind your shiny teak desk in your plush corner office, you casually look into your coffee cup, and decide that it's half-empty."

He could feel the tenseness in her body, hear the pain in her voice. "Your teak desk? Your corner office?" he asked, knowing the answer.

She nodded her head, fighting back sudden tears. "I can still feel how that stupid, random thought stunned me—like a shot to the solar plexus. I stared into that damned cup for a full hour, as the world of Ransom Computers revolved around me, my mind filled with memories of Dad, while I blubbered like a baby."

Daniel didn't know what to say, didn't know how to comfort her, but he shouldn't have worried. Joey scrubbed at her eyes and looked up at him, smiling widely. "And you know what I finally did, Daniel Quinn? At the end of that hour I blew my nose, pushed my sixteen-position chair clear of my teak desk, stood up and walked away. I walked away from my Rolodex, my hefty expense account, my awe-inspiring title of production executive, my rosy lucrative future—and I didn't even bother to look back. I've never looked back!"

If Daniel had been surprised before, now he was astounded. Joey had been an executive—a top executive. He had known she was intelligent, but he'd had no idea just how intelligent. If she had told him she'd had a breakdown from stress, or lost her job due to a takeover—that he could have understood. But to work yourself that far up the ladder, and then just walk away! "You're kidding!" he exclaimed with astonished condemnation, staring at her. "What did you do then?"

Joey was feeling pleased with herself, so pleased that she was finally pouring out her story some other way than by scribbling it onto page after page of her journal.

"Well," she went on, "the first thing I did was check my bank account and make arrangements for Andy's junior and senior year of college. Then, for two years I roamed the country in my trusty baby-blue Mercedes, stopping where I wanted, camping out on a moonlit beach in San Diego or checking into a bed and breakfast in some sleepy Maine town. Driving long country miles with the top down and the wind blowing through my hair—just plain old reveling in the simple joy of being alive, hokey as that sounds."

She had also kept a hit-or-miss journal of her travels—not that she so forgot herself as to reveal this to Daniel—recording her thoughts, her feelings, her reactions to the people and places she had seen. She had soaked up her experiences like a thirsty sponge soaks up water, and promised herself that never again would she be so foolish as to put herself in a box of anyone else's making, no matter how well padded it might be.

"Then, two years ago," she concluded aloud, "when Andy graduated and told me he wanted to be a singer, we hatched the idea of Abbott's Aristocrat Limousines, to keep body and soul together until Andy gets his big break."

"I see," Daniel said, not seeing at all. "And once Andy gets this big break of his—what then? Do you sell the limousine service and use the profits to hit the road once more—like some sort of gypsy—until you run out of money again?"

Joey snuggled down once more. "That's a good point, Daniel. I don't really know how to answer that. I might, if the spirit moves me. I guess I'll just take it one day at a time."

Suddenly she was wildly reaching for the arm of the swing and trying to maintain her balance as Daniel leaped to his feet. "I don't believe it! You're as bad as he is!" he exclaimed, glaring down at her.

"As bad as whom?" she asked, totally confused. What *was* Daniel's problem?

"That's *who*!" Daniel shouted, his motives for correcting her grammar no less childish than his son's had been. "And Wilbur Langley—that's who! And to think I believed you'd be a good influence on Richie. A lady chauffeur with orange sunglasses and purple high-top sneakers! If Wilbur's Peter Pan, then you're Tinker Bell! My God, I ought to have my head examined!"

Joey watched, openmouthed, as Daniel stomped his way across the wooden porch and slammed across the gravel driveway to his car. "That's *woman* chauffeur, you chauvinist!'' she shouted after him, throwing herself back against the porch swing and pumping it back and forth furiously. A moment later Daniel and his Cadillac roared off into the night.

Chapter Six

Hi, Joey! Did you and Dad have a good time last night? Dad overslept this morning, and now he's grumbling through the house like a bull with a sore paw, or at least that's what Mrs. Hemmings says. She's pretty funny, once you get to know her, and she's going to let me help her make some chocolate chip cookies tonight after I give her a hand with the dishes. If you want, we have time to go to the garage for a while. I want to show you something.''

Joey blinked twice, disbelieving both what she was hearing and what she was seeing. Richie Quinn was smiling as he came down the front steps and approached the limousine, his tall, too thin body clothed in its usual mismatched, psychedelic mayhem. He was actually smiling, and his enthusiastic voice was light and cheery. What a difference a day could make! Had Mrs. Hemmings slipped something into his cocoa?

"You're pretty chipper for six in the morning, Rich," she said, readily falling into step beside him as they walked around the side of the house to the garage. "What's up? Your horse finish first yesterday at Belmont?"

Richie turned to grin at her. "Dad told you about that, huh? No, it was nothing like that. Billy Simpson came by last night on his bike. It's a ten-speed. I'm going to get one just like it."

"Billy Simpson from the baseball team?" Joey asked weakly, her head reeling.

Richie nodded, then took a small hand control from his back pocket and pointed it at the garage, electronically opening the oversize overhead door. "He lives about a mile away, didn't you know that? Jeez, and you're his coach. Anyway, he came over last night and we hacked around for a while."

"Hacked around?" Joey stepped into the garage, where she could see the large, six-foot-wide blue target Richie had painted on one wall. Now she knew how Alice had felt when she tumbled into Wonderland. She searched the garage with her eyes, looking for the tea party.

Richie picked up his fielder's glove from a small workbench and bent to retrieve a whiffle ball from the floor. "On the computer, Joey," he supplied helpfully. "Billy has some great games he brought with him. Terrific graphics. You like computer games, Joey?"

"I used to think I did," she replied, smiling wryly, thinking of her years at Ransom, "but I don't play them anymore. What's that?" she asked, pointing to the center of the target, which was painted in the shape of a particularly fearsome, leering face.

"He's Kreppo, the evil king of Wanjung. I guess you haven't played computer games in a while. It's the best game out right now. I painted him there for inspiration. It was Billy's idea, actually, and it really works. I think I'm getting pretty good at hitting him."

Joey looked at the narrowed, slanted eyes, pointy bared teeth and cauliflower ears of King Kreppo. "He's a real incentive giver, I'll say that for him. Okay, let me see what you can do."

Richie positioned himself behind a strip of tape he had secured to the floor and wound up, delivering the ball straight to King Kreppo's chops. "All right!" he shouted, turning to Joey. "Is that rad, or what?"

"Rad?" Joey repeated, longing to find Billy Simpson and give him a smacking kiss square on his freckled nose. Almost overnight, Richie Quinn had been turned into a ten-year-old. "It's *awesome*!"

"It's *late*, Ms. Abbott," corrected a frigid voice from the driveway. "If it wouldn't be too much to ask, might we be on our way?"

Joey looked across to where Daniel was standing, attaché case in hand and condemning scowl on his face, then back to Richie, who was winding up for another pitch, his smile still intact. "Some mad scientist must have crept in here last night and done a personality transplant on these two," Joey muttered under her breath. "Be right there, Daniel," she called more loudly, waving goodbye to Richie as her tight-lipped employer turned on his heels and disappeared around the corner of the house.

"So much for hoping Daniel would have calmed down by this morning. I have a feeling today is going to be terrific. Just peachy-keen terrific from beginning to end," she grumbled fatalistically, sliding behind the wheel and twisting the key in the ignition.

Deliberately leaving the glass partition in the down position, she strapped on her seat belt and put Esmeralda in gear, the limousine gliding effortlessly down the curved drive and out onto the narrow macadam road. Sneaking a quick look in the rearview mirror, she saw that Daniel, dressed for success once more in a sedate business suit, was already hard at work in the backseat, a computer spreadsheet opened across his lap. She fought down the nasty urge to turn on the heater, for the chill in the air was a tangible thing on this warm June morning.

Joey didn't know whether to be angry or amused. Not everyone agreed with her life-style—she'd learned that long ago—but she'd never had anyone respond quite so negatively as Daniel had last night. She would have thought she had baldly announced she was a mad killer on temporary leave from the state penitentiary, for the fear she had seen on Daniel's face as he had accused her of being "just like him."

Him. Wilbur Langley. As she merged Esmeralda into the early-morning commuter traffic on the thruway, Joey turned her thoughts to Wilbur, and the facts she

had gleaned from Daniel's comments about his father-in-law and late wife. All right, so Wilbur was a
feckless, reckless, if somewhat elderly playboy. So
what? He'd earned the right to have some fun, hadn't
he? After all, he had run Langley Books for a long
time.

Granted, she thought, as she put on the turn signal
to move into the passing lane, Wilbur had overstepped
the role of loving grandparent in his treatment of Richie. Joey could agree with Daniel on that one point at
least, if the bus ticket incident was to serve as an ex-
ample of Wilbur's idea of what constituted a good
time. But life with Wilbur Langley would be much like
life with the fictional Auntie Mame, and every child
should have at least one delicious Auntie Mame in his
life.

Joey concluded that Daniel must believe he was
seeing history repeating itself with Richie, assuming
that Daniel blamed Wilbur for Veronica's lack of maturity. Her gray eyes narrowed as another thought hit
her. "Wait a minute, Joey, old girl. Back up a few
paces and think about this," she muttered beneath her
breath. Did Daniel really believe that *she* was another
Veronica? Was it Richie he was protecting, or himself?

"Why, that—" she began, suddenly very angry.
How dare he think that! Who did he think he was,
anyway? She was *so* responsible! Hadn't she raised
Andy single-handedly when her father died? Hadn't
she taken care of Andy economically? Hadn't she been
a good employee? She had thought Stan Ransom was

going to have a spasm when she told him she was quitting her cushy job, for crying out loud! Yes, she had been good. She had been damned good!

And now she was damned good at heading up Abbott's Aristocrat Limousines! Just who did he think he was, this Daniel Quinn, to look down his patrician nose at her life-style? "Like he's so simon-pure," she groused, slanting another quick look into the rearview mirror.

Why hadn't she realized all this last night, as she lay awake in her lonely bed, trying to make some sense of Daniel's desertion? She'd been so busy worrying about him, worrying about Richie, that she had forgotten to take care of Numero Uno.

"Tinker Bell, is it?" Joey gritted from between clenched teeth as her knuckles turned white on the steering wheel. How dare he insult her that way, hurt her that way? Well, she wasn't hurt anymore. Now she was angry!

Her foot rode the gas pedal heavily as she continued her garbled train of thought. If she was such a bad influence, just how did Daniel explain the sudden change for the better in his son, Richie? "Yeah," she whispered meanly, "how do you explain that, Mr. Holier-than-thou Quinn? After all, whose idea was it to sign Richie up for baseball? Answer me that, you miserable—" she gritted, pulling into line at the tollbooth for the New Jersey Turnpike.

"It's a good thing you're not in any danger of falling in love with that hypercritical stick," she complimented herself, reaching for a tissue to wipe at her strangely moist eyes. "Well, that's it! I'll hold on until Andy gets back, but then I'm outta here! And if Daniel Quinn doesn't like it, well then, he can darn well take the bus!"

This is ridiculous! Daniel folded the spreadsheet with more energy than care, stuffing it into his attaché case before flopping back against the seat and crossing his arms over his chest. He glared out the side window for a moment as the limousine stood still in line at the tollbooth, then directed his glare to the back of Joey's cap-covered head. *This is bloody ridiculous!*

Less than twenty-four hours ago they had laughed together across a dinner table. Less than twenty-four hours ago he had held her, kissed her, smelled the perfume of her hair, listened to her dreams—and done a little dreaming of his own. *Now she's talking to herself a mile a minute up there and I'm sitting back here, my spine aching with righteous pride and indignation. It's like a scene out of a bad novel—a very bad novel.*

What a difference a day makes! Oh, God, that's trite! "But true," he remarked quietly as the limousine inched closer to the tollbooth. Would this ride never end? How was he going to keep up this pretense of not caring—twice a day, three days a week, for six months? "It's impossible!" he hissed, shifting uncomfortably in the seat.

And then there was the problem of Richie. Only a fool could be unhappy with the change in Richie, the change that was taking on signs of being nearly miraculous.

Richie liked Joey. Joey was one of the Bulldogs'
baseball coaches. Joey was driving him to New York
three days a week. Adding Tuesday and Saturday
games and Thursday practices, staying away from Joey
Abbott—and keeping Richie away from her—would be
like trying to remove a fifty-cent wad of chewing gum
from the bottom of his shoe.

Couldn't she even take a hint? He had barked at her
in the garage, the only words he'd spoken to her since
he ran away last night like a spooked teenager, yet she
had answered him politely, and with a smile. She hadn't
said a word to him since she slipped behind the wheel—
not "how are you?" or "did you manage to remove
your tail from between your legs yet?" or even "drop
dead!" No, she'd just sat up front, with the dividing
glass opened, keeping her eyes on the road and her
mouth shut—except for the heated conversation she
seemed to be holding with herself. It was just like a
woman to behave herself, making the man look even
more stupid than he already felt!

"Why the hell don't you take off that stupid cap?"
he heard himself bark loudly, wishing he had known he
was going to say something that ridiculous, so that he
could have choked himself first.

He watched as Joey took the ticket from the auto-
mated tollbooth but did not step on the gas. Instead,
she slowly turned her head to look at him, her expression maddeningly blank. "Why the hell don't I just
sprinkle you with pixie dust and make you disap-
pear?" she asked just as the tinted glass divider slid up,

cutting off all further hope of conversation until the limousine delivered him to Langley Books.

That night, when he reentered the limousine, the first thing he noticed—after noting Joey's stony expression as she held the door for him—was that the glass divider was still in the raised position. It was a long, silent ride home to Saucon Valley.

Joey wasn't at the Thursday practice, having been hired to drive three women to Philadelphia for the day, so that Daniel had to wait until Friday before seeing her again. By then, he had a plan to permanently remove Joey Abbott from his life, if not from his dreams.

Daniel's solution to his dilemma had a name. As a matter of fact, it had several names, like Roseanne, and Muffy, and Stephanie and, if none of them worked, even the ever lovely Ursula. Yes, he thought meanly, mumbling his grudging thanks as Joey held the door for him as he climbed inside the limousine Friday morning, Ursula would really put the capper on it.

"Please leave the glass down today, Joey," he said as pleasantly as his clenched jaws allowed before the car door could be slammed shut and he lost his chance to speak to her again.

"You're the boss," she replied, smiling brightly, just as if they had never argued. *Not that we actually have,* he reminded himself with a slight sense of shame. *I've acted like an ass, and she let me. But the fact remains. Joey Abbott is poison to me, and the worst sort of influence on someone as susceptible as Richie. I'm doing the right thing. I know I am.*

He watched as Joey gracefully slid behind the steering wheel, looking as fresh and pretty as the proverbial daisy, and even more beautiful this morning than she had seated across the dinner table from him in the restaurant. *But then flighty butterflies are always lovelier than worker bees,* he reminded himself with a strangely unsatisfying smirk.

"Are you free tonight, Joey?" he asked once they were on their way.

Joey's heart did a small flip in her breast. So, Daniel was having second thoughts, was he? Well, never let it be said Joey Abbott was one to hold a grudge. "Yes, Daniel. I'm free this evening," she replied, turning her head to smile at him.

"Good," Daniel declared, nodding his head. "In that case, I'll be bringing someone home with me this evening, to spend the weekend. I'd like you to drive us to dinner—someplace romantic. Roseanne prefers seafood if my memory serves me correctly."

"Roseanne?" Joey whispered under her breath, hoping Daniel didn't notice Esmeralda's slight swerve toward the passing lane. "Seafood, you say?"

"That's right. Seafood. You know—those finny things that live in the ocean. Any suggestions?"

Joey had several suggestions—none of them repeatable. She chanced a quick peek in the rearview mirror and saw the smug look on Daniel's face. Her eyes narrowing, she rapidly debated the consequences of tossing him out on the shoulder of the highway and leaving him there.

The bank manager had called late Thursday afternoon, telling her that her loan was on the way to being approved, thanks to the Quinn contract. She could salvage her pride by tossing Daniel out on his ear, but that would mean she could also wave that second limousine bye-bye at the same time. She might consider herself a free spirit, but she certainly didn't believe in lopping off her own nose to spite Daniel Quinn's smirking face!

She knew what he was doing, of course. He was attracted to her, just as she had been attracted to him. Now he was going to prove to her just how little she meant to him by going out of his way to throw other women in her face. It was pitiful. *Men are such little boys,* she told herself, ordering a smile onto her own face. *Well, two can play at this game!*

"Stokesay Castle in Reading is a lovely restaurant," she heard herself saying politely. "It's about a forty-five-minute ride each way, so it makes for a nice evening out. I take couples there all the time and I've never had a complaint."

Daniel expelled his held breath in defeat. Her hesitation had allowed him to hope he had scored a direct hit with the mention of Roseanne's name. Joey hadn't even flinched. Maybe he was reading too much into a single candlelit dinner and one soul-shattering kiss. But there was still Richie to consider, he reminded himself, refusing to acknowledge the pain Joey's obvious lack of jealousy caused him. If he could make Joey hate him, she'd get out of Richie's life as well.

"Stokesay Castle?" he repeated, deliberately employing a world-weary New Yorker tone of laughing disbelief. "That's a pretty ambitious name for a small town restaurant. What does it have—a prefab turret and a couple of stone fireplaces?"

"Stokesay Castle," Joey began in her most professional voice, "is a 1931 recreation of the original Stokesay Castle built in the thirteenth century and still standing today in Shropshire, England. Mr. George Bear Hiester, obviously a very rich and very besotted gentleman, had it built as a honeymoon cottage for his bride, duplicating the original down to the last hand-hewn beam and leaded window. It sits on top of a high hill just outside the town of Reading, where it commands a delightful thirty-mile view of the countryside."

"You sound like a professional tour guide, but we'll play it your way," Daniel said, wanting to do nothing more than reach into the front seat and strangle her, or kiss her. Compromising, he moved from the wide backseat to the smaller seat located just behind the glass partition. "How did this great castle come to be a restaurant? Did poor old George lose it all in the stock market crash?"

Joey kept her head facing front and her eyes on the road, doing her best to ignore the heady scent of his cologne. "It would appear that George's bride had little taste for castles, even castles with three hundred-amp electrical service and all the modern conveniences," she informed him politely, then added, "Roseanne? Roseanne who?"

"What an ungrateful woman Mrs. Hiester must have been," Daniel answered, allowing his fingers to stray to the nape of Joey's neck, where they lightly teased at the sensitive nerve endings so that she was forced to press her head back against his hand. "Roseanne Philpot. She's a dress designer. She thinks Richie is adorably refreshing and extremely intelligent and usually shows up with an educational toy in tow."

"Bully for Richie," Joey countered, having successfully rid herself of Daniel's teasing fingers. "And bully for Roseanne. I'll call the manager for reservations once we get to New York. We'll probably have to drive straight to Reading, unless you object. I'll have you booked for the Blue Room. It's 'sumptuous.'"

"How efficient of you," Daniel complimented gruffly. Looking around himself in some surprise, he wondered how he had forgotten his good intentions enough to be sitting directly behind Joey, touching her like a servant boy stroking the hem of the queen's robe.

"I have my moments," Joey responded dryly, seeing Daniel's face reflected in the rearview mirror and doing her best not to laugh at his baffled expression. "Now it's up periscope time, before you forget how much you loathe me. Your hand, Daniel?" she prompted smartly as she moved to press the button that would raise the glass partition. "Move it or lose it!"

Still holding open Esmeralda's passenger door, Joey occupied herself with glaring at Daniel's retreating back as he walked toward the double glass doors of the Sixth Avenue office building.

"Once around the park, if you please, Joey darling," she heard a voice say just as a blur of royal blue whizzed past her to enter the backseat of the limousine.

She leaned over the top of the car door to get a good look at her unexpected passenger. "Wilbur Langley!" she exclaimed as he winked at her from the interior of the limousine, waggling the fingers of one hand at her in greeting. She noted his obviously expensive suit. "Congratulations. I see you've officially entered your blue period. Now, what do you think you're doing?"

"Why, Joey, dear," he responded happily, "I thought I was clear enough. I'd like a leisurely spin around the park, of course. Then I thought we'd stop at Tavern on the Green for a spot of liquid refreshment. Unless you'd rather elope with me to Barbados. I'm flexible. Oh!" he exclaimed. "I've just had a lovely thought. Could I possibly ride up front with you? I've never done, you know, and it might be easier to hold a conversation that way. That is, if it isn't against some chauffeuring law, or something."

"A law like that was made to be broken, Wilbur, if it even exists. Besides, I'm off duty until five-thirty." Joey held out her hand to assist Wilbur's exit from the backseat, then walked around the limousine with him to unlock the passenger door and open it with a flourishing bow.

Joey inched Esmeralda back into the heavy Manhattan traffic and headed for the park, her usual good humor resurfacing after the trying silence she'd endured ever since raising the glass partition between herself and her maddening employer. A dose of Wilbur Langley, she decided, might be just what the doctor ordered.

"How's that son-in-law of mine treating you, my dear?" Wilbur asked after a moment. "Richie was not his usual lucid self on the telephone last night, mumbling and grumbling about his father not allowing him to mention your name in his presence. What did you do—slap his face when he made a pass at you at dinner?"

"How did you know we went out to—oh, Richie told you. You two are worse than a pair of old biddies hanging over a back fence. And no, I didn't slap his face."

"But he did make a pass," Wilbur inserted slyly, folding his hands across his chest in satisfaction. "I always said that boy had a good head on his shoulders."

"Only until I knock it off," Joey responded tightly, turning the limousine into a parking garage. "Let's walk, Wilbur. I've been driving for hours, and I'd like to have my mind entirely free to talk to you. I think it's safer that way, and I don't mean traffic-wise."

Wilbur scrambled from the car first, to help Joey exit from the driver's side, and she couldn't help noticing the strange look the two of them got from the young parking attendant. "Thank you, kind sir," she said, turning back to leave her cap on the front seat and pick up her sunglasses. "Shall we adjourn to the park?"

They walked in companionable silence for some minutes as Joey rethought her decision to consult with

Wilbur Langley about Daniel. After all, he was the man's father-in-law—as well as the man Daniel had described as an irresponsible Peter Pan. How could she tell him her problem without letting it slip that Daniel also heartily disapproved of him?

They stopped to listen to a jazz trio who had set up their instruments at one of the entrances to the park, then lingered to watch a magician play tricks on passersby who volunteered to help him with his show. Joey laughed out loud as Wilbur pointed out a huffing, puffing nanny chasing after her charge, who was in the process of making a run for it across the wide lawn.

Finally, Wilbur pulled her over to sit beside him on a bench, as a group of joggers, led by a high-stepping coach, took possession of the pathway. "Such a pointless waste of good energy, don't you think?" Wilbur asked, pointing to the sweating, straining crowd as they jogged past.

"I think it would be easier to just skip dessert," Joey said, agreeing with him. "So, Wilbur, how's Richie? I haven't seen him since Wednesday morning."

Wilbur leaned back against the faded wooden bench, rubbing his hands together. "He's fine, I'm happy to report, although I must tell you that both you and I have dropped a notch on his favorite people list. Some young upstart named Billy Simpson now holds that most coveted spot. I'm quite distraught. I think I'll have to purchase season tickets to the Yankees, perish the thought, just to win my way back into his good graces."

Joey leaned over and kissed the man's cheek. "You old fraud. You don't fool me for a moment. You're glad Richie's found a friend. I don't know why Daniel's so set against—um, that is—"

As Joey's voice trailed off in confusion, Wilbur patted her hand, saying, "That's all right, my dear. It's no great secret that Daniel thinks I'm a bad influence on my grandson. I most probably am, you know."

Joey squeezed his hand in hers. "Well, Wilbur, don't feel like the Lone Ranger. Daniel thinks I'm a bad influence, too."

"On whom? Richie—or Daniel?"

Joey smiled at Wilbur's quick perception. "Does the name Roseanne Philpot ring any bells?" she asked as they rose once more and walked leisurely across the grass, the bright sunlight warming their shoulders.

"Roseanne Philpot? He's pulling her out, is he?" Wilbur marveled, a low whistle hissing through his perfectly capped teeth. "The boy is desperate, isn't he? Funny, I would have thought he'd go for Ursula. She's only half as smart as Roseanne, but she's built like a— well, never mind that. Congratulations, my dear, and welcome to the family. We're sorely in need of an infusion of fresh young blood."

"Whoa, Wilbur!" Joey exclaimed, stopping in her tracks. "Don't you think you're presuming a bit much? I like Daniel, very much. But we hardly even know each other. Not only that, but we're barely speaking. I wouldn't go planning the wedding if I were you. Besides, who says I'd even *want* to get married. I'm quite happy as I am."

"Of course, my dear," Wilbur agreed smoothly, drawing her hand through the crook of his arm. "You're right to be prudent. After all, you're not even thirty, are you? There's plenty of time. I suppose this means I shall have to instruct Richie to cancel the orchestra?"

Chapter Seven

She was very tall, very thin and very, very beautiful. She was dressed from blond head to shapely calf in some redder-than-red flowing thing that defied description and probably cost half as much as Esmeralda. If Roseanne Philpot was to be the competition, Joey thought with a grimace, Daniel believed in pulling out all the stops. Fortunately for Joey, her worry was wasted, and short-lived.

Roseanne, Joey soon learned, considered herself to be a liberated woman. She had clawed her way to the top of the designing world through her own efforts—except for the two million dollars in "seed money" she had acquired thanks to her ex-husband, Phineas "The king of ripple potato chips" Philpot. But, as she considered her marriage to have been comparable to living in a war zone, she comforted herself with the thought that she had earned every penny of that two million dollars.

Being an independent woman, Roseanne obviously admired any woman who took her life into her own hands, broke new ground and dared to go where only men had successfully gone before. Daniel, in his intention to demonstrate to Joey just how little he needed her, had made a serious blunder in forgetting Roseanne's dedication to the feminist movement.

"A woman chauffeur?" Roseanne had exclaimed as she and Daniel walked arm in arm across the wide pavement toward the open limousine door. "How fascinating! Daniel, you didn't tell me your limousine service was broad-minded enough to hire women drivers."

"Actually, Ms. Philpot," Joey interjected politely, smiling directly into Daniel's suddenly smoldering eyes, "I'm not just a driver. I am the co-owner of Abbott's Aristocrat Limousines." *Stuff that in your briefcase and tote it,* her eyes told Daniel.

Roseanne dropped Daniel's arm in order to take Joey's right hand in both of hers, pumping it up and down enthusiastically. "That's absolutely wonderful! I applaud you. I can't tell you how much I admire women willing to take charge of their own lives. Please, leave the partition down so that you can tell me all about it on our way to this castle Daniel has told me about."

By the time Esmeralda was tooling down the New Jersey Turnpike, Roseanne and Joey were on a first-name basis, and Daniel was slouched in his seat, sulking. He did come in for some reflected praise at one point, as Roseanne congratulated him for being sure enough of his own masculinity to hire a woman driver, but for the most part he found himself politely, and totally, ignored.

When they arrived at Stokesay Castle, Roseanne asked Joey what she would do to occupy her time while they had dinner, and Joey explained that it was her custom to sit in the kitchen with the cooks. "Sometimes I sample whatever's on the menu, but most of the time I just nibble on some pizza until it's time to go," she told them as Roseanne stood in the cobbled courtyard, marveling at the immensity of the restaurant grounds.

"But that's horrible! Daniel! You'd be a party to this sort of archaic, chauvinistic discrimination?" Roseanne exclaimed, turning on Daniel, who suddenly found himself feeling like Simon Legree sending little Eliza out onto the ice floe.

"Boy oh boy, Daniel," Joey teased in a low voice, moving to stand beside him. "However do you sleep nights, you monster?"

Roseanne wiped her hands briskly against each other, dismissing any such nonsense. "Well, Daniel, I won't have it, do you hear me? Relegating Joey to the kitchens, like some medieval serf? I had thought better of you, Daniel, truly I had."

"Yeah," Joey intoned softly, shaking her head. "We had thought better of you, Daniel."

Daniel spoke to her out of the corner of his mouth. "You're enjoying this, aren't you?" he accused, looking down at her condemningly.

"You got that in one, bunkie," Joey retorted happily as Roseanne took her arm and led her into the castle, leaving Daniel to follow or to stay as he chose.

Joey missed the first game of the Bulldogs' season, as she would miss most of the Saturday games, having leased Esmeralda as the bridal car in a local wedding. She hated missing the games, but weddings were always fun, and brides and bridegrooms were very undemanding passengers, who were always more interested in each other than in telling her how to drive.

Sunday morning, as she used the local car wash's vacuum to remove the last of the confetti and rice from the tufted velvet upholstery of the backseat, Steve Mitchum, the Bulldogs' coach and the owner of the car wash, filled her in on what had happened at the game.

"Billy Simpson held them to a six-hitter, but he walked seven batters, and that really killed us," Steve informed her, yelling so that he could be heard over the sound of the vacuum's motor. "Still, we only lost 10-8 to last year's league champions, so there's hope for us yet. It's a long season."

Keeping her head carefully averted, Joey asked, "I guess the game was too close to let any of the scrubs in for an inning?"

"If you mean did Richie Quinn get in, the answer is no," Steve returned, winking at her, "but he did do a bang-up job keeping the stats. That kid adds faster in his head than I do using a calculator. Not only that, but he has a memory like an elephant.''

"In what way?" Joey asked, surprising herself at how her heart had filled with near-maternal pride at Steve's praise of Richie.

"He could remember how many pitches Billy threw, and what pitch he used to strike out their cleanup hitter in the fourth inning—you name it and Richie knew it. Like I told Daniel—that kid's got a home with me any time he wants one!''

"*As* I told Daniel," Joey corrected, too quietly for Steve to hear, proving to herself that Richie had begun to rub off on her as well. "Daniel was there?" she questioned, keeping her voice deliberately light. "I know he has company this weekend, so I didn't think he'd be able to make it."

Steve eyed her closely. "You mean the blonde?" he asked, helping Joey replace the vacuum on the shelf. "He brought her along. She told me the kids' uniforms are all wrong—something about flow, and natural motion being more important than pinstripes. But she did compliment me for having Melissa Hancock playing third base. Strange woman, don't you think? I was surprised to see Daniel with her. He seems more your type."

Joey smiled up at him. "And what type is that, Steve? Really, I'd like to know."

Steve looked at her uncomfortably, then spread his arms. "Jeez, I don't know, Joey. Just more—more *touchable*. Yeah, that's it. Touchable. And more fun. You're a lot of fun, Joey."

She fished in the pocket of her jeans for her car keys. "That's me all right, Steve. I'm a lot of fun. A real barrel of laughs. But would you want to settle down with me?"

Steve spread his hands in front of him, as if warding off attack. "Hey, Joey! I'm a married man."

"Good morning, Steve." Joey and Steve both turned to see Daniel walking toward them, having turned his car over to one of the attendants. "I thought I'd get my car washed before driving Roseanne back to New York. Good morning, Joey," he added, seemingly as an afterthought.

"Good morning, Daniel," Joey answered with more civility than welcome, sliding behind the wheel. "Well, Steve, I gotta go. I'm picking up a client at the Newark airport at three. Daniel, I'll see you tomorrow morning."

She had turned the key in the ignition before Daniel's knock against the side window caught her attention. She lowered the window in time to hear him say, "Isn't there some way we could combine our efforts? After all, it's only nine o'clock. There would be plenty of time to drop Roseanne on Park Avenue and still get to Newark before three."

Joey tried to hide her smile, and failed miserably. As wars went, it seemed that she had conquered him with ridiculous ease. Clearly this was surrender. Well, never let it be said that Joey Abbott was a poor winner. "That seems reasonable, Daniel," she agreed quickly. "I can be at your house in half an hour."

"Great!" Daniel said, Joey recognizing the tone of victory in his voice too late to do anything about it. "I'll see that Roseanne is ready for you. I'm sure you two still have plenty to say to each other, even if you did talk for three hours over dinner Friday night. Now I'll have the whole afternoon free to take Richie and Billy Simpson to that movie they want to see. Thanks a lot, Joey. Just add the trip to my tab."

That was how Joey got to spend two long, frustrating hours listening to Roseanne Philpot's philosophy of life as they drove to New York City in a sudden pouring rain. And that was how Joey Abbott learned that, when it came to love and war, Daniel Quinn certainly subscribed to the old saying that warned "all is fair."

Monday's trip to the city was, as Joey was to write later in her journal, a complete, undiluted disaster, with a capital *D*. She was still bristling at Daniel's high-handed attitude of the day before, and Daniel, who seemed to be a sudden convert to the feminist movement, treated her more like one of the boys than most boys she knew. He had even slapped her on the back companionably as he climbed into the backseat of the limousine.

The ride to Manhattan had been accomplished in stony silence—which more than pleased Joey, who wasn't feeling all that talkative that morning. But the trip home was one long headache, beginning with the moment the left rear tire blew out just as the limousine pulled onto the New Jersey Turnpike.

She cursed once, softly, under her breath, steered Esmeralda onto the shoulder of the road and got out to inspect the damage. There was no doubt about it. The tire was as flat as three-day-old seltzer. With her hands jammed onto her hips, she allowed another short, unlovely descriptive phrase to pass her lips.

"I may be way out of line here," Daniel interposed silkily, leaning his tall frame against the side of the car, "but I don't think flat tires respond well to having their legitimacy questioned."

Joey turned to look at him, standing at his ease, his hip against the car door, his arms crossed over his chest and an infuriatingly pleased smile on his face. "Oh, shut up!" she exclaimed, kicking the flat tire and bruising herself in the process so that she spent the next few moments hopping about on one foot, rubbing at her abused toes. "If you say one more word, Daniel Quinn, I'll bop you. I swear I will!" she warned tightly as his mouth opened to, she was sure, point out that it was equally useless to try kick-starting the tire back to life.

"I was only going to ask you if you've got a spare in the trunk," Daniel told her, unable to suppress a short laugh at her predicament. "A male driver would have one. A tire jack, too."

Joey shook her head slowly, feeling her blood beginning to boil. "Oh, you'd love it if I didn't have a spare, wouldn't you? You've been just dying to show me up as a poor driver, ever since that first day. Admit it, Daniel. You just hate it that I'm self-sufficient—that I don't need a big, strong man to take care of me."

He pressed a fist against his chest, his expression innocently incredulous. "Me? You'd think that of me? Is that what you and Roseanne decided? Do you really think I'm one of those Neanderthal types who goes out to get the meat, while the little woman keeps the cave warm? Well, you couldn't be more wrong."

"Oh, yeah, sure," Joey grumbled as a large tractor trailer whizzed by, sending up a cloud of dust that drifted over Esmeralda, Daniel and herself like a shroud.

"You don't believe me, do you?" Daniel asked as the dust settled. "How can I convince you? Let's see— you believe that I'm a chauvinist, and I believe I can remember accusing you of being irresponsible. As I see it, we can settle both problems quite easily."

"Really," Joey said, wondering what had been wrong with her brain to ever make her believe she had been in any danger of losing her heart to this man.

"Yes, really," Daniel said, opening the car door. "I can get back into this car right now, proving that I feel you are my equal, and therefore equally as capable of changing a tire as any man. And you can change the tire, proving to me that you're more than a silly, irresponsible little girl, playing at life. Simple, isn't it?"

Joey's eyes got very wide. "You—you're going to get back in the car, and let me change this tire by myself?" she squeaked in disbelief.

"Can't you handle it?"

"*Of course* I can handle it!" she shouted above the roar of late-afternoon rush hour traffic. "With one *hand* tied behind my back, I can handle it! But I'll be darned if I'm going to jack up your weight as well as Esmeralda's. Go sit on the bank until I'm done."

Daniel smiled and saluted her smartly before walking around the back of the limousine and seating his long frame on the grass embankment, fully prepared to watch his chauffeur change a flat tire.

"Hi, Sis. Miss me?"

Joey had raced into the house to grab the telephone before the caller could hang up, having heard it ringing as she trudged wearily toward the porch steps. "Andy!" she exclaimed, her heart leaping at the sound of her brother's voice. "I just got in. You don't know how good it is to hear from you!"

"Yeah? Well, you almost didn't hear from me, sister mine. The phone must have rung at least ten times. I was just about ready to give up hope. Why didn't you put the answering machine on before you went out? How are prospective customers supposed to get through to us? Maybe I'd better hop the next plane home and take charge of things, before you put us out of business."

"You take charge? Har-de-har-har, *brother mine*," Joey answered, reaching over to pull a kitchen chair closer to the telephone so that she could collapse her aching, weary body onto it. "*You*'re going to take charge? You couldn't possibly mean the same Andy Abbott who once booked us for three weddings on the same day?"

"Why can't you ever forget that, Sis? We pulled it off, didn't we?" Andy complained, the whine in his voice sounding clearly in her ears. "So, how are you doing, anyway? Have you heard from the bank?"

Joey glanced down at her grease-covered blouse, dusty skirt and shredded panty hose, then held up her right hand to inspect the three broken fingernails that had been sacrificed while lifting the spare tire into place. "Me? Hey, I'm doing great. Just fine, honest. Couldn't be better. We'll get the final word from the bank in a few days, but it looks good at this end."

"Gee, Sis, don't sound so overwhelmed with happiness." There was a small silence on the other end of the phone. "It's Monday, isn't it? You sort of lose track of time on the river, you know. Today's a Quinn day. Is he giving you any trouble?"

Joey felt the beginnings of frustrated tears stinging at the back of her eyes. "No, Andy, he's not giving me any trouble. You've just caught me at a bad time. I had a blowout with Esmeralda on the way home."

"Gee, that's tough. Too bad it didn't happen when Mr. Quinn was with you. He would have fixed it for you."

Immediately Joey bristled. "You, too!" she shot back with some heat. "Just what makes you men think a woman can't change a simple flat tire? It's not like performing brain surgery, for heaven's sake. This is *my* business, and tire blowouts are a part of it. I'm not playing at this job, you know."

"Uh, sure, Joey. Of course. Sorry about that," Andy mumbled, clearly confused. "Hey, the guys are calling me, Sis. I gotta go now. I'll call you again later in the week, okay?" Before Joey could answer, her brother had broken the connection.

She replaced the telephone receiver and dropped her head into her hands. "What's the matter with me?" she groaned on a sob. "I've changed a dozen tires in my life. Why does it bother me so much that Daniel didn't help me with this one? What is that man doing to me? Why do I want him to see me as a woman, but treat me like a lady—like someone who's special to him? Why isn't this game we're playing funny anymore?"

That night, just as Joey was about to go to bed, there was a knock at the kitchen door.

"May I come in?" Daniel asked as she peeked at him through the curtains of the glass-topped door. He was dressed casually in slacks and a knit shirt, and he was holding a small bouquet of flowers in front of him, as if for protection.

Her fingers fumbled nervously as she struggled to release the dead bolt and let him in. Clutching the top of her short cotton robe to her breast, she stepped back two paces, her bare toes curling against the cool linoleum floor. "Hello, Daniel," she said in a small voice, hating herself for avoiding contact with his eyes.

Daniel moved inside, still holding the flowers. He was nervous, and he disliked the feeling. Joey looked beautiful, all freshly scrubbed, her nose shiny, her dark hair clinging to her shapely head in soft, damp ringlets. She smelled like soap and shampoo, and something deep inside him twisted into a knot, then squeezed itself tight.

"I would have been here sooner, but it takes longer when you have to kick yourself all the way," he said, holding out the bouquet.

Joey looked up at last, and he could see that her gray eyes were overly bright. "For me?" she said, her voice low and faintly hoarse. She took them gingerly, doing her best not to let their fingers touch. "I'll put them in water."

Daniel followed along behind her as Joey walked toward the dining room in search of a vase. "About this afternoon," he said in a rush, eager to have his apology over and done with as soon as possible. "I don't know what got into me, Joey, honestly I don't. I'd skin Richie alive if he ever treated a woman that way. Please forgive me. I acted like a complete—"

"Yes. Yes, you did," Joey said, cutting him off. "But I accept your apology. There," she said, dropping the flowers into a milk glass vase that had belonged to her mother, "this will do. Now all they need is a nice long drink of water. Excuse me, please."

Daniel frowned for a moment, then stepped to one side, allowing Joey to pass by him back into the kitchen. Once more he found himself following her, like a puppy dog hoping for a treat. "Would you believe I got them at the supermarket? Mrs. Hemmings was right—they sell everything in those places nowadays."

"Mrs. Hemmings is very nice," Joey said, placing the vase in the middle of the kitchen table.

Oh, this is going great, Daniel thought, grimacing. After Joey sat down he sat as well, carefully choosing a chair on the other side of the table. "Do you think we can call a truce, Joey?" he asked, leaning forward to move the vase to one side in order to see her better. "I don't think there can be any winners in our little war. Besides, Richie has been asking about you."

"I haven't seen him since last week," Joey told him, and he noticed that she hadn't said either yes or no to his offer of a truce. "I was disappointed that he wasn't awake when I picked you up this morning."

Daniel nodded, eager to get on to a safer subject, and for once Richie was a safer subject. "He spent last night with Billy Simpson, and they went to Hershey Park today with Billy's parents. He just got home a little while ago."

"Hershey Park is a nice place," Joey commented dully. "The whole town smells like a chocolate bar, and the rides are fun. Richie and Billy seem to be hitting it off very well. I'm glad, for both of you."

Daniel reached across the table to take hold of Joey's hands, stopping her in the midst of shredding a second paper napkin. "They never would have met if you hadn't blackmailed Rich into joining the Bulldogs. If I haven't thanked you for that yet, please let me do it now."

He was left with his empty hands stretched across the table as Joey suddenly sprang to her feet to fill the tea-kettle and put it on the stove. "I don't want your thanks, Daniel. I would have done the same for any child. You don't owe me anything."

The hem of Joey's bathrobe barely skimmed the top of her thighs as she bent forward to turn on the burner and Daniel swallowed hard, knowing he had to talk before he could act. Yet acting was just what he wanted to do. The memory of Joey's kiss still burned in him, and he had to know if his disgust at her cavalier way of looking at life had been successful in putting out the fire.

As Joey stood with her back to him, waiting for the water to come to a boil, Daniel rose and walked around the table to lay his hands on her shoulders. "I hurt you the other evening, didn't I?"

"Hurt me?" Joey repeated hollowly. "Don't be silly. How could you have hurt me? I'd have to care in order to be hurt. I'm going to have a cup of tea. Do you want tea or coffee?"

"Joey," Daniel whispered huskily, using his hands to turn her around to face him. "You have to understand. If Veronica showed me nothing else, she showed me that I need stability in my life. It's great to see every cup as half-full, every cloudy day as partly sunny. I'll bet you even do crossword puzzles in ink—the eternal optimist. But to work hard for something and then just throw it away on a whim, to take off across the country like some—some—"

"Some irresponsible butterfly? Some overage Tinker Bell? Some footloose, fancy-free gypsy? What's the matter, Daniel? Don't tell me you're suddenly at a loss for words."

"Damn it, Joey, will you just shut up and let me talk!" Daniel fairly shouted, giving her slim shoulders a small shake. "Don't you understand anything? I'm attracted to you. It doesn't take a rocket scientist to know that there's some sort of chemistry going on between us—something that's been going on between us since that first day."

Joey's eyes were liquid smoke as she replied shakily, "Yes, Daniel. I know. But that doesn't change anything. I'm not what you want in a woman. I'm too much like Veronica, too much like Wilbur."

Daniel crushed her against his chest, holding her to him tightly. "You're nothing like Veronica. Veronica cared only for herself. You care about people, Joey, maybe too much. Don't ever say you're like Veronica."

Joey gloried in this new closeness, her hands raised to clutch at Daniel's forearms as she melted against his strength. "That leaves Wilbur," she pointed out honestly, mentally slapping herself for not letting well enough alone. Daniel was here, in her house. She was here, in his arms. When would she ever learn to keep her great, big, stupid mouth shut?

Rubbing his cheek against the top of her head, Daniel closed his eyes and thought about Joey's admission that she wouldn't be opposed to selling the limousine service she had worked so hard to build in order to go out and experience life, in the same way she had done after leaving Ransom Computer. "You were just answering a hypothetical question that night," he reasoned, as much to himself as to her, "and I overreacted. You wouldn't really leave the business.

You had two years to get the wanderlust out of your system."

Joey pushed against him until she stood at arms' reach, glaring up at him, her eyes no longer gray smoke, but gray ice. "Says who—or is that *whom*? Do you think I want to spend the rest of my life chauffeuring other people around?"

Daniel was losing her, and he knew it. "No, of course I don't think that," he hastened to answer, trying without success to draw her back into his arms. "You'll want to marry someday, and have children. If you want to continue working, you'll want to work at something more conventional."

"And who makes you the authority on what's conventional?" she shot back at him. "If your precious Roseanne could hear you now her dark roots would turn white! Here!" she shouted, grabbing the flowers from the vase and handing him the dripping stems. "Take your stupid peace offering and get out of here!"

"With pleasure!" Daniel yelled back at her, holding the sopping flowers as he turned toward the door. He stopped just as his hand touched the knob and turned back to her. "You know, I'm not quite sure what we're arguing about, but I'm damned sure of one thing—*you're crazy!*"

It wasn't until he was halfway home that Daniel realized that he had goofed—again.

Chapter Eight

Tuesday arrived, and with it came a drenching, day-long rain, relieving Joey of the necessity of seeing Daniel at Richie's baseball game. Wednesday brought back the sun, and a surprise that went a long way toward restoring Joey's sense of humor.

Wednesday, Joey learned as she picked up Daniel at his office at five-thirty for another long, silent ride to Saucon Valley, was to bring her sweet, petite Muffy Arnstein.

Muffy was the most female female Joey had ever seen, a woman so appealingly helpless she would have made Roseanne Philpot gag at the sight of her. Dressed in chiffon ruffles and drooping bows that accentuated her full bosom, generous hips and infinitesimal waist, her hair was black as midnight, while her magnolia-pure skin and cherry lips reminded Joey of Holly-wood's version of Snow White.

Although they were both pretty much the same height, Muffy made Joey feel as if she had been somehow suddenly catapulted back to pre-puberty. If Daniel sincerely believed that a female's "womanliness" could be measured in direct proportion to her bra size, Joey decided, then Muffy Arnstein was the perfect woman.

Muffy didn't walk. Oh, no. Muffy bounced, her sky-high heels clicking against the pavement as she approached the limousine, hanging on to Daniel's arm as if she could not conceive of crossing such a dangerous stretch of territory without his manly protection.

Joey tore her fascinated gaze away from Muffy's bouncing bosom in order to look at Daniel and gauge his mood. It was infuriatingly smug. He was grinning from ear to ear, just like a little boy who has found all the Christmas presents his parents had hidden in the attic, and she knew that if she'd had something heavy in her hand at that moment, she would have bopped him over the head with it without a second thought.

"This way, Muffy," she heard Daniel saying as he guided the woman toward the curb, and Esmeralda.

"Oh, Danny!" Muffy exclaimed in a high, childlike soprano as Joey opened the back door to allow the seemingly glued-together couple to enter. "Don't tell me this little ol' gal drives this big ol' car for you! I must say, I am impressed. Why, I just shudder to think of my ever being brave enough to even think of doing such a thing. Is she going to be driving us *all the way* to that delicious castle you told me about over lunch?''

"Yes, *Danny*, what is it to be?" Joey asked quietly as Daniel approached the limousine and unstuck his companion long enough for her to slide across the backseat. "Do I take you all the way, or can I drop you somewhere—preferably over the side of the Phillipsburg Bridge into the Delaware River. But not to worry, Danny boy. I have a sneaking suspicion dearest Muffy would float."

Daniel spoke through clenched teeth. "Just cut the cute act and drive. I called ahead, and we have reservations at Stokesay Castle for eight o'clock. And this time," he added meanly, "*you* eat in the kitchen."

"Yes, master," Joey answered, tipping her cap. "Anything you say, master. Oh," she added, just about to turn away, "would you care for a gas mask? Muffy's perfume might just eat up all the oxygen back there."

Daniel didn't answer her, but merely slid onto the backseat and pulled the door shut behind him. His left arm was immediately grabbed by Muffy, who continued to hold on to him with the tenacity of a pit bull until they reached Stokesay Castle more than two hours later. His head was ringing from her constant, inane chatter, and his self-respect was dragging in the mud.

Joey opened the door for them once the limousine had glided to a halt in the courtyard, then took herself off to the kitchen, where she sat perched on a high stool and allowed the chef to feed her delicious samples of all that was offered on that night's menu.

Daniel, however, ate nothing. All he could do was sit across the table from Muffy and think of poor Joey, forced to sit in a steamy kitchen and eat greasy pizza. It was possibly the longest night in his recollection, and he didn't breathe easily until he had released Muffy into Mrs. Hemmings's care and locked the door to his study behind him, intent on pouring himself a double Scotch on the rocks.

"Damn!" he exclaimed into the darkness as he lifted the lid of the ice bucket. "Talk about poetic justice." There was nothing inside the bucket except a small puddle of warm water.

Joey was free to attend the Bulldogs' Thursday practice, but Daniel only dropped Richie off and drove away, Muffy by his side. Joey watched as his car disappeared around the corner, refusing to admit that his defection bothered her personally—it was just that he was letting down the team.

"Hi, Joey," Richie called as he loped across the infield to her, his fielder's glove dangling from his right hand. "Dad says he's sorry he has to skip practice, but he's got to take Muffy to Philadelphia to visit her brother. Boy, is she an airhead! I think Dad's really lost it this time. I think I liked it better when he worked all the time. Grandpa says he's drowning, but not to worry about it. I hate it when Grandpa's cryptic, but it makes him happy. Are you going to be here for the whole practice? Coach Mitchum is going to give me a few pointers on playing the outfield."

Joey assured Richie that she had the entire after-noon free, then complimented him on how well he was keeping the statistics for the team. "I was just looking over the book, Richie. I've never seen it in such good shape."

"It is stimulating," Richie agreed, shrugging as if to say it wasn't really important, "but I'd rather play right field. Billy's been helping me with my hitting. You know, it's really all basic physics. I mean, there's the force, the action and the opposite reaction. It's just a matter of finding the right combination, the right equation—"

Holding up her hands as if to ward off his explana-tion, Joey laughed, pleading, "Please, Rich, you're taking all the romance out of the game!" then quickly changed the subject. "So, how is your grandfather? I saw him one day last week in New York, but he could have flown off to Timbuktu since then, knowing Wil-bur."

"He's still in New York," Richie told her, waving to Billy as he climbed out of a station wagon and headed onto the ball field. "He wanted me to come for a visit, but I just don't have the time right now. So I invited him to come to Saucon Valley for a visit."

"Do you think he will?" Joey asked, trying but failing to picture Wilbur Langley in the suburbs.

"He says he thinks he might have to get up-to-date on his shots first, but he'll think about it," Richie an-swered, laughing. "Well," he went on as Steve Mit-chum clapped his hands to call the team to order, "here we go again. Joey, do you think you could take me home? Billy's mom said she would, but it's been a long time since I've had a ride in Esmeralda, and—''

''I'd love to,'' Joey answered, suddenly realizing how much she had missed Richie, and assured that she wouldn't be running into Daniel at the Quinn house, as he would have his hands full with Muffy. She grimaced, silently reworking that last thought in her head.

Once the two-hour practice was over, she and Richie drove to a nearby ice cream parlor to spend some time talking over hot fudge sundaes before heading for home. Richie successfully delayed the trip further by begging Joey to drive him to the local computer store, where he pulled a crumpled wad of bills from his pocket to pay for a new game for his computer. It was nearly supper time before she pulled Esmeralda into the sloping curved driveway in front of the brick Colonial.

The front door opened almost immediately and an irate-looking Daniel Quinn bounded down the steps, yelling, ''Where the hell have you two been? Do you have any idea what time it is? I've been to Philadelphia and back, for God's sake! Billy Simpson's been home for over an hour! I was ready to call the police.''

Joey's cheeks puffed out as she expelled her breath sharply with the realization that she had managed to look bad in Daniel's eyes once more. How was she to have known that Daniel was going to drive to Philadelphia, drop Muffy on her brother like a hot potato and race home again, just in time to point out, yet again, how flighty and irresponsible she was?

"I'm sorry, Daniel," she said, hastening to get out of the car and save Richie from his father's wrath. "It's my fault entirely. I should have called Mrs. Hemmings to say we'd be late."

"No, *you* shouldn't have," Daniel interrupted. "That would have been the logical, sensible thing to do. But you're a free spirit, aren't you? Free spirits don't look at clocks, or worry about anything but enjoying the moment."

"It's not Joey's fault, Dad," Richie cut in, stepping in front of her protectively. "I'm the one who wanted to stop at the computer store. Don't be angry with Joey."

Both Daniel and Joey looked at Richie, who was actually volunteering to take the blame when he could just as easily have gotten off the hook, and neither one of them could think of anything to say. Luckily, at that moment, Mrs. Hemmings appeared in the doorway to ask Richie if he thought he could set the dinner table from where he was standing.

Uncomfortable silence reigned on the driveway for several moments after Richie trotted into the house, a silence that Joey finally broke. "There are times I almost believe that the Richie I met on Forty-second Street and the Richie who just ran inside to help Mrs. Hemmings are two entirely different boys. You must be very pleased. Saucon Valley seems to have been just what the doctor ordered. Daniel?" she prompted when he didn't answer her.

"Muffy was a mistake, Joey," Daniel admitted quietly at last, staring down at her intently. "So was

Roseanne, when you come right down to it, but Muffy was the worst. The very worst. I had to drive her to Philadelphia fast, before I strangled her with her own hair."

Joey felt a small thrill of triumph race through her body, but quickly stifled it. "She was certainly—um— *different*, I'll say that for her."

Daniel sniffed, shaking his head. "I haven't been called Danny since the third grade. I'd only known her from seeing her at Wilbur's parties. Roseanne, too." He looked directly into Joey's eyes as another thought hit him. "Wilbur's got some strange friends, do you know that?"

"And you haven't even gotten to Ursula," Joey pointed out, remembering Wilbur's mention of that particular name the day they had strolled together through Central Park. "He seemed to think she might be a winner."

"Ursula?" Daniel repeated, his brow furrowing in confusion. "You know about Ursula? When did you talk with Wilbur? Damn that man! Why can't he mind his own business?"

Walking over to lean a hip against Esmeralda's front fender, Joey reasoned, "You and Richie *are* his business, at least in Wilbur's mind. I know I'm overstepping myself saying this, Daniel, but maybe it's time you put the past to rest and worked with the present. Your father-in-law cares about you. You might try working with him, instead of against him. It's stupid to be in competition with him over your son's affection."

Daniel's eyes narrowed for a moment in quick anger, then his expression softened. "You're right, of course. I have been measuring Wilbur against his raising of Veronica, and barely giving him a chance. He may not be a typical gray-haired grandfather, but he wouldn't have been able to gain so much influence over Richie if I had been paying enough attention to my own son." His features hardened again. "But that doesn't give him the right to start meddling in *my* life! That's what he's doing, isn't it—trying his hand at a little matchmaking?"

"If you mean, is he trying to get the two of us together, yes, I think he is," Joey returned just as angrily. "But don't worry, Daniel. I wouldn't have you if you got down on your knees and begged me!"

"And you'd hold your breath a long time before I'd even think of it," Daniel told her, moving away from the limousine. "We're totally incompatible—even more than Roseanne or Muffy."

"Or Ursula?" Joey shot back at him, already heading around to the driver's side of the limousine.

"Especially Ursula!" Daniel shouted. "I don't want any woman in my life right now. I've just found my son, and that's more than enough for me right now. The last thing I need is some idiotic woman to drive me insane. When the hell is your brother getting back?"

Taken slightly off her guard, Joey answered him automatically, "Andy? Next Tuesday. Why?"

"Then we only have tomorrow and Monday to get through," he pointed out, his voice strangely quiet.

"Starting Wednesday morning, I want to see Andy behind the wheel. You got that?"

"In spades!" Joey yelled, opening the car door.
"Tell Richie I said goodbye," she added before starting the engine and sending Esmeralda fishtailing down
the drive, the tires spitting out angry bits of gravel in
their wake.

By Monday morning Joey was beginning to think of
the tinted-glass partition that divided the front seat
from the passenger compartment as her own private
Berlin Wall, complete with snarling guard dogs.

After dropping Daniel on Sixth Avenue she parked
Esmeralda at a local garage and walked to Wilbur's
penthouse, using her smile and a carefully folded five
dollar bill to bribe the doorman into calling upstairs to
see if Daniel's father-in-law was at home. He was, and
she rode up on the elevator with her hands wrapped
tightly around the flat brown paper bag she had
brought with her, wondering just what she thought she
was doing.

"Joey, darling!" Wilbur greeted as the door of the
elevator whispered open and she stepped onto the shiny
parquet floor that had replaced the ankle-deep white
carpeting. He kissed her on both cheeks, then took
hold of one hand and held it out in front of her. "Let
me look at you. How difficult it is to imagine you in
anything but this ridiculous uniform. You should wear
chiffon, my dear. Baby-pink chiffon."

"Like Muffy?" Joey asked, grimacing.

"Good Lord, no!" Wilbur responded, dropping her hands. "Never, ever like Muffy. Unfortunate child, I think she was off redoing her lip gloss when the brains were being handed out. Forgive me. I can't imagine what I was thinking, comparing you to Muffy Arnstein. I guess I shall just leave the dressing of you up to your own discretion, although I would hope you'd seriously reconsider the purple sneakers. They just aren't *in* anymore, you know."

Joey looked around the massive living room, nodding her head in appreciation. The room was furnished entirely in the English country style, with plenty of overstuffed blue-and-white-chintz sofas, and a gigantic faded Oriental carpet cushioning her footsteps. "I like this new phase much better, Wilbur," she complimented sincerely. "I believe even Daniel would approve."

Wilbur looked around the room himself, as if seeing it for the first time. "I had an extra room converted into a computer room cum bedroom for Richie. The walls are covered with baseball pennants and pictures of Einstein and some other bearded fellow the boy favors. I think he'll be pleased. Now, sit down. What can I do for you?"

Joey sat down on one corner of the sofa that faced the fireplace, the paper bag now clutched tightly in both hands. "This is crazy," she said, not really speaking to Wilbur. "I really shouldn't be doing this. I'm taking advantage of you. I'm so ashamed of myself."

Wilbur leaned back against the soft cushions, eyeing the flat package. "Let me venture a guess, my dear. You've written a book, and now you want my opinion as to whether or not it's any good."

Joey's head shot up in surprise. "How—how did you know?"

He leaned over to remove the bag from Joey's nerveless fingers. "It's a sixth sense we publishers develop over the course of several decades. What is it—romance? Mystery? Horror?"

Wrinkling her nose, she said, "Fictionalized personal experience—the very worst thing of all to pull off successfully, at least according to everything I've read on the subject. I've already been turned down several times, including a form rejection letter from Langley Books." She tried to take the package back from him. "I really shouldn't be wasting your time with it, Wilbur, but—"

"But you'll force yourself to, right?" he teased, lightly slapping her fingers away before sliding the rubber-band-held sheaf of papers from the bag. "Have you shown this to Daniel?"

She shook her head. "Daniel wouldn't understand," she explained. "I've told him a little bit about it in a way, and he thinks—well, to be perfectly honest, he thinks I'm slightly deranged. He'd never give a book that attempts to justify my life-style an even chance." She made a face. "That sounds a little self-righteous, doesn't it? Daniel's entitled to his own opinion."

"Daniel's entitled to be horsewhipped," Wilbur stated firmly, reaching into his pocket to retrieve a snow-white handkerchief, which he handed to Joey. "Here. Wipe your eyes. I'll read your book."

Joey dried her eyes and smiled at Wilbur. "Only if you promise to be brutally honest."

"Brutal it is," he agreed, laying the manuscript to one side. "Now, dearest Joey, since my son-in-law is too blind to see what's in front of his face, how about I try my hand at monopolizing your time? How does luncheon at the Plaza sound to you?"

"The Plaza sounds absolutely lovely, Wilbur," Joey said honestly, allowing him to help her to her feet. "Thank you."

If Carl Sandburg's Chicago fog tiptoed into town on little cat feet, New York's fog roared in on a Mack truck, thick and fast, and mowing down anything in its path. Traffic inched along the streets of Manhattan, the entire city brought to its knees by the swirling, dense mist.

At five-thirty, after spending the afternoon with Wilbur, Joey carefully nudged Esmeralda into a parking space just outside Daniel's office building. Her eyelids narrowed as she searched the pavement for some sign of him. She hoped he would be on time because, at the rate things were going now, she doubted they would be clear of the city in less than an hour.

The rear passenger door opened and closed before she could register the fact that he had found Esmeralda in the sea of limousines and mist. He knocked sharply against the glass partition, motioning for her to lower it. "How fast can you get to the Allentown-Bethlehem-Easton International Airport, Joey?" he began without preamble.

"To ABE?" she asked, frowning. "Wouldn't Newark Airport be closer? Besides, what planes would be taking off in this pea soup?"

"None," he answered shortly. "That's why Courtney Blackmun's flight from the West Coast is being diverted to the ABE airport. Her plane will be landing there in a little over two hours. I told Harry, her agent, we'd pick her up and take her to my house for the night. Now, if you've no further questions, I suggest we get on with it. Or do you want me to drive?"

"No, I don't want you to drive," Joey sneered back at him. "I don't *have* a death wish." She raised the glass partition and steered Esmeralda out into the swell of private cars and fog.

It was only after thinking about it for a few minutes that she regretted her quick sarcasm, for she really would have liked to learn more about Courtney Blackmun, a novelist whose work she truly enjoyed.

They had only traveled about forty miles when Daniel knocked on the glass partition once more. "It's really slow going, isn't it, Joey?" he commented, leaning his forearms against the top of the rear-facing seat so that his head was close to hers. "Person to person—and not chauvinist to helpless female—would you like me to take over the wheel for a while? Not that you aren't doing beautifully, because you are. As I told you before, you really are an exceptionally good driver."

"Thank you. They let me take off the training wheels a while ago. But I don't mind driving, Daniel," Joey answered honestly, turning her head to give him a quick, forgiving smile, "though it would be nice to have someone to talk to while I try to keep my eyes on the white line in the middle of this mess. This is unusual, a fog this heavy. It wasn't forecast. It reminds me more of the California coast than New Jersey." She hoped her reminder of the West Coast would bring Daniel's mind back to Courtney Blackmun.

Daniel's mind was very obliging. "That's where Courtney's coming from—San Francisco, to be precise. She just finished up the first leg of the publicity tour for her new book. Have you read it yet?"

Joey shook her head. "I've been meaning to get it, but I haven't had time."

"I'll get you a copy. I'm sure I have one at home. Would you like it autographed?" Daniel didn't know why he was going out of his way to be so nice to Joey, but talking about Courtney kept his mind busy, and away from thoughts of asking Joey to pull Esmeralda onto the shoulder of the road so that he could climb into the front seat with her until the fog lifted. Or, he thought, smiling, she could climb into the backseat with him. Surely together they could find some mutually satisfying way to pass the time.

"I'd like that," Joey said, turning on the windshield wipers, for the fog was lifting as it began to rain.

"You'd like what?" Daniel asked vaguely, his attention all centered on the soft curve of Joey's neck.

"An autograph. I'd like a Courtney Blackmun autograph," she repeated helpfully.

"Oh, yes. Courtney," Daniel said, remembering his bestselling author. "She'll be staying overnight, and catching a plane to New York tomorrow morning."

"I have the day free, Daniel, if you'd like me to drive her. The airports will be jammed tomorrow after this," Joey offered shakily, feeling his fingers rubbing lightly against her nape and realizing that she was suddenly finding it rather difficult to breathe.

"I guess so," he answered absently. "Joey," he said before he could talk himself out of it, "there's a rest stop just ahead. Pull over."

"Pull over?" Joey swallowed, hard.

"Pull over, Joey," Daniel repeated huskily, his lips softly brushing the delicate skin just beneath her right ear, "*please*."

He was out the passenger door and reinstalled in the wide front seat before she could put the gear lever into the park position, and she was in his arms before either of them could remember that they really weren't speaking to each other.

His hands were hard and demanding as they ranged up and down her back, his lips wildly searching, his body pressed tightly against hers. Her mouth opened beneath his as she welcomed his possession, her eyes tightly closed, her heart pounding loudly in her ears, so loudly that she could not hear her saner self telling her that she was being a fool.

"Oh, Joey," Daniel breathed at last, holding her against his chest, "it's still just as good. Maybe even better. I'm not going to fight it anymore. You can drive Esmeralda to Alaska and back, or climb mountains in Peru, or run for president—I don't care. Just please let Richie and me tag along with you."

Tears filled Joey's eyes. This was surrender, but they were both winners. "I don't want to do any of those things," she told him, suddenly realizing that she was speaking the truth. "My cup became completely full the moment I met you. There's nowhere else I'd rather be, than to be with you. Nothing else I'd rather do than hold you forever and ever."

He pushed her slightly away from him, looking down into her eyes. "You mean that, don't you? My God, you mean it. Oh, Joey!" he groaned, claiming her lips once more as he pulled her from behind the wheel and onto his lap.

Several minutes later, when the defroster finally cleared the steamed windows, Daniel steered Esmeralda back out onto the highway, Joey sitting close beside him, her head pressed comfortably against his shoulder. "I haven't necked in a car since high school," she told him, rubbing her cheek against his suit coat.

"I should think so. It's damned uncomfortable, if you want my opinion, and way too public. We'll deposit Courtney with Mrs. Hemmings and the two of us can continue on to your place," Daniel told her as they crossed over the bridge at Phillipsburg and entered a fog-free Pennsylvania. "We have a lot to talk about."

Joey lifted her head to smile into his eyes. "Talk about, Daniel?" she asked, pretending to be shocked. "You mean you really want to *talk*?"

Daniel lifted one eyebrow and leered at her. "What do you think?"

Chapter Nine

Joey wasn't quite sure what was going on, hadn't been sure of much of anything ever since Daniel ordered her to pull Esmeralda into the roadside rest stop—but she was more than willing to "go with the flow." As a matter of fact, she was pretty sure she would need to resort to plastic surgery in order to have the inane smile wiped from her face. She was so happy she almost believed she could hear herself purring.

This was what life was all about—what it was really all about. This was what her father and mother had had and taken for granted, what her father had missed so desperately when his wife was gone, the regret he must have carried with him to his grave. This was what he had wanted for his children. Love. Complete, total love. A reason to believe that life was, even in the worst of times, always more than half-full.

She hadn't found this sense of completeness climbing the corporate ladder at Ransom Computers. She hadn't discovered it hiding in the laid-back far West or waiting for her on the warm shores of southern Florida. She hadn't met up with it as she drove Esmeralda everywhere and arrived nowhere, meeting people and learning and growing, but never really discovering anything.

She had been going about it all wrong. Happiness wasn't a place, or an occupation, or the freedom to see a sunrise or eat ice cream for breakfast. Happiness was loving, and being loved.

There was nothing of this sort of love, this complete happiness that was worth any pain, in the manuscript she had given Wilbur. This particular, mind-blowing revelation was a whole other book, a whole other world. A world that just might be too private for her ever to want to share it with anyone else.

Daniel hadn't said he loved her, she realized as, following her directions, he steered the limousine toward the off ramp nearest the airport. She wrinkled her nose. Neither had she, if it came right down to it. *There's plenty of time for hearts and flowers,* she decided, reluctantly moving away from the comfort of his shoulder in order to check her hair in the rearview mirror. *Right now it's enough that he knows he can't live without me.*

"Lord, that's smug!" she exclaimed out loud, running a finger across her kiss-swollen bottom lip.

"What?" Daniel asked, before turning onto the road leading to the terminal. "What's smug?"

"Smug?" Joey repeated in sudden panic. "Did I say smug? I meant *smudged*. It's my lipstick. My lipstick is smudged."

"Your lipstick, my dearest chauffeurette, is *missing*," Daniel informed her with what could only be called a note of triumph in his voice. "Now help me find a parking place for this boat. Courtney's plane should have landed a half hour ago."

"What does she look like?" Joey asked as she raced across the parking lot, taking two steps to each of Daniel's longer, ground-eating strides. "I mean, I've seen her picture on the back of her book jackets, but those things don't really tell you anything. Attila the Hun would look good after three hours of hair and makeup, photographed through cheesecloth, and with a wind machine running."

Daniel took her hand as he entered the terminal and stopped for a moment, trying to decide which way to go. "She'll be easy to recognize, Joey. Courtney will be the one with a mountain of luggage, and steam coming out her ears. Maybe her nose, too."

"Temperamental?" Joey asked, adjusting her cap with her free hand while trying to catch her breath.

"Talented," Daniel corrected, his pace increasing once more as he spotted his bestselling author sitting cross-legged on an oversize Gucci suitcase directly beneath a No Smoking sign, a lit cigarette dangling from her long, slim fingers. He released Joey's hand. "You don't have to hang on to your cap. We've lucked out. I don't think Mount Saint Courtney is going to blow her top."

Joey looked across the terminal to the baggage claim area, immediately knowing that she was looking at Courtney Blackmun. She would have recognized her even if she had never seen her picture. Courtney Blackmun *looked* like a writer, from her designer luggage, to her sleek, sophisticated ivory shantung suit and deep emerald blouse, to her long, silk-clad legs, to the cloud of cigarette smoke making a blue-gray halo around her artfully windblown ebony shoulder-length curls. *"Wow!"* she said, impressed. "She looks more like one of the heroines in her books than the heroines in her books."

"Yeah," Daniel said quietly out of the corner of his mouth as he waved at the writer. "Just don't gush, okay? Courtney hates gushers. Hello, Courtney!" he said in his cheeriest voice as he and Joey halted in front of her. "Been waiting long?"

"I never gush," Joey grumbled, feeling as if she had just been relegated to the role of teenage rock-star groupie. "I wouldn't know how to gush."

"Daniel," Courtney said coolly, rising to her full height, which put her a good half foot above Joey, who first looked up at the woman, then down at her own feet, to gasp in dismay as she discovered that she was still wearing her purple high-tops. "Who's your little friend?"

Go ahead, Daniel, Joey cried inwardly, longing to tug on his sleeve and feed him lines. *Tell her who your little friend is. Tell her that we're late because you spent a half hour necking in a limo on the New Jersey Turn-pike. Come on, Danny boy, sock it to her!*

"Joey is my chauffeur, Courtney," Daniel said, stooping to kiss the author on the cheek. "Courtney Blackmun, allow me to introduce you to Joey Abbott. Joey, give me a hand with these bags, will you? Courtney's been waiting here long enough."

Joey watched as Courtney's left eyebrow—one perfectly sculpted brow of a perfectly matching pair—rose a fraction. "Your chauffeur, Daniel?" she questioned, looking at Joey levelly. She held out her right hand, taking Joey's in a firm grip. "How nice to meet you, Joey. You must lead an interesting life."

Courtney's green eyes could see inside and read her soul, Joey was sure of it. The woman had done no more than touch her hand, and she was convinced the writer now knew her entire life's story. Joey retrieved her hand quickly, wanting to find a lead helmet with which to cover her head so that Courtney couldn't use her X-ray eyes to read her mind as well. "Nice—nice meeting you, Ms. Blackmun," she heard herself stammer as she quickly gathered up the two smaller pieces of luggage and headed for the door.

She got as far as the limousine before realizing that Daniel had the keys to the trunk in his pocket. Resisting the urge to throw the cases to the ground and then stomp on them, she laid them down gently and turned to see Courtney and Daniel taking their good sweet time in joining her, Courtney's arm comfortably twined around his as they laughed at some private joke.

"I could be invisible, for all that man cares," Joey told herself, trying but not succeeding in working up a head of steam. She wasn't angry. Not really. She was hurting, badly, and she couldn't understand how Daniel could run so hot and cold—kissing her passionately one moment and treating her like an employee the next. A not very important employee, too.

"It's a good job I didn't tell him I love him," she muttered, leaning against Esmeralda's rear fender. "He might want me, but when itch comes to scratch, I'm still just a freewheeling chauffeur, and not good enough to acknowledge in public. Steamed-up cars and the privacy of my house in the dark—that's all I'm good for. Well, if that's what he thinks, he can just go take a flying leap!"

Daniel deposited the heavy suitcase beside the trunk and produced the key chain, handing it over to Joey. "Sorry about that. I forgot I still had them," he said sheepishly. "Courtney, let me get you settled in the backseat and we'll be on our way in a moment. All in all, you've had a pretty rough day."

"I'll show him a rough day," Joey groused under her breath, hefting the largest suitcase into the trunk. "Courtney Blackmun in full sail will look like a toy boat in the Central Park lake compared to the rough day I'm going to give him!"

"Hey, that's heavy. I would have handled it," Daniel said, coming up behind her, leaning over her to shift the suitcase to one side of the trunk. He lifted the two smaller bags and dropped them beside the suitcase. "You should have waited."

Joey's eyelids were narrowed as she looked up at him. "Really?" she asked, putting her hands on her hips. "And how long would I have to wait to be introduced to Courtney? Or was that never part of the program?"

Daniel was confused, and his expression clearly reflected it. "What do you mean, Joey? I introduced you."

"What do you mean, Joey?" she recited in a singsong voice, her belligerent chin nearly stabbing him in the chest. "I *mean*, Mr. Quinn, when am I going to be introduced as something other than your chauffeur? Admit it! You had another moment of madness back there on the turnpike, and now you've come screeching back to your senses. You don't have to knock me over the head with a brick, you know. I can take a hint."

"What in hell are you talking about?"

"I'm talking about how you're ashamed of me, of how you *really* feel about me."

Daniel's face went dead white, something Joey had already realized happened only when he was very angry. He reached out to take hold of her shoulders. "You idiot!" he accused. "There's a time and a place for everything. And the middle of that terminal wasn't either of them. All I wanted to do was get Courtney out of there before the fire marshal fined her. You want commitment, Joey? You want acknowledgment? I'll give you an introduction that'll knock your socks off. Come with me!"

Before she knew what was happening to her she was standing beside the open door to the passenger compartment and Daniel was announcing in a loud voice that brooked no argument, "Courtney Blackmun, I'd like to introduce you to Joey Abbott."

"Yes, we've already met," Courtney responded sweetly, smiling up at Joey in that Cheshire cat way that Joey had already learned to fear. "Was there something else you neglected to tell me, Daniel?"

"Yes, there is. As Joey just pointed out to me, it seems that I somehow forgot to tell you that Joey Abbott is not only my employee, but also the most infuriating, independent, mind-destroying, *exasperating* female I have ever met—and I'm crazy about her."

Joey leaned against his side, smiling down at Courtney. "He's crazy about me," she verified simply. "Isn't he cute?"

Courtney reached into her purse and withdrew a slim gold cigarette case. "He's utterly adorable," she said, lifting a cigarette to her lips and lighting it with a jeweled lighter. "If you'd like to kiss the bride, Daniel, please do it quickly. Then, if you're both done with telling me what I already know, and it wouldn't be too much bother, I'd like to go somewhere quiet and take a long, hot bath."

"I think you must have believed Courtney's publicity, Daniel," Joey said two hours later, turning the sizzling hamburgers on the gas grill with a large spatula. "She couldn't have been more sweet."

"That's because she's smoking again," Daniel told her as he sat at his ease in a lawn chair, feeling oddly aroused by Joey's efficient movements as she worked in shorts, tank top and an oversize apron carrying the notice: "It's my kitchen and I'll cook what I damn well please."

"What does smoking have to do with it? And stop leering at me. Richie's here, remember?"

"She's always more mellow when she lapses back into her single vice. The cigarettes also mean that she's ready to get down to work again. According to Courtney, smoking makes writing easier—something to do with stimulating and concentrating the creative brain cells. Between books she quits."

"Which explains why her publicity tours are always such a headache, right? I mean, what with the withdrawal symptoms and all that?" Joey asked, lifting the hamburgers onto already prepared buns. "Well, I just think it's nice that she's in her room writing down ideas for her new book, and you're free to be here with me."

Daniel took the plate she handed him, holding it under his nose and sniffing appreciatively at the charcoal-broiled aroma. "I'm also free to be away from Mrs. Hemmings, who has been giving hourly bulletins on the amount of smoke floating through the upstairs, quoting more statistics than the surgeon general. That's why Richie is with me. She didn't want him exposed to side-steam smoke."

"Umm, I think I like you in shorts," Joey commented, sitting cross-legged on the grass with her hamburger and leaning her back against his bare leg.

"You've got great legs, for a man. Straight, and not too fuzzy. And that's side-*stream* smoke, Daniel."

"Not if your name is Mrs. Hemmings," Daniel explained, ruffling her short curls. "Uh-oh. I think we've got company. Behave yourself, woman."

Richie appeared from around the corner of the house just as his father took the first bite of his hamburger. "That's right, don't call me," he complained, not really upset. "Just let me stay in the barn playing with the kittens—and starving to death. Boy, Joey, that smells good," he complimented, grabbing a loaded plate for himself. "Hey, and real homemade potato salad, too. This is really neat. Picnicking. Could you guys see Grandpa eating from a paper plate?"

"Only if it was at the Plaza and a tuxedo-clad waiter was holding it for him," Daniel said, making Joey choke on a bite of potato salad. He pounded her lightly on her back until she stopped coughing. "Joey, didn't you say there was a Phillies game on television tonight?"

The conspiratorial tone of his voice had Joey hiding a smile behind her hand as she answered his question. "Yup. It started ten minutes ago, as a matter of fact. There's a lefty pitching."

"Really?" Richie remarked around a mouthful of hamburger. "I think it's really interesting the way lefties can make the curve ball break left to right as it travels downward across the plate. That's why they're particularly effective against left-handed batters, you know."

"Yes," Joey broke in wryly as she heard Daniel suppressing a laugh, "we know."

"I figure," Richie went on, undaunted, "that if I can just study their motion long enough, and then feed the data into my computer, I can figure out a way to beat 'em. Do you mind if I go inside and watch?"

"Be my guest," Joey answered in a strangled voice as Daniel's leg shifted behind her, so that she fell into the cradle between his knees.

"Thank God! I thought he'd never leave," Daniel said once Richie had gone, taking a second hamburger along with him as he ran up the porch steps, the wooden screen door slamming shut behind him. "If he thinks he can actually beat a good left-hander with a computer, he needs more help than I can give him."

"Oh, yeah?" Joey pushed herself back up to a sitting position and turned to look him in the eye. "I've seen what a computer can do, Daniel, my friend. Five bucks says he goes two for four the next time he's up against a lefty. Put up or shut up. And help me clean up around here before it gets too dark to find everything."

"Pretty cocky, aren't you? And pretty bossy, too. Cocky and bossy," he mused, shaking his head, and not moving another muscle. "That's a bad combination. Maybe I'd better round up Richie and get out of here while the getting's good. What do you think?"

Joey grabbed his hands and pulled him to his feet. "I think he doth protest too much," she told him, growing more sure of herself and his love for her with each passing moment. "Now come here and kiss me. I've been a good girl ever since you got here, dragging your son in tow as protection. You owe me, Daniel Quinn. It's time to pay up.''

"Oh, is that right?" he asked teasingly, lifting her at the waist to deposit her on top of one long picnic bench, so that they were at eye level with each other, their bodies pressed tightly together from hip to thigh. Raising her hands, he twined her arms around to the back of his neck, laughing as he added jokingly, "Why don't you try to make me?" Then he felt his muscles tense as he watched her smile slowly leaving her face. "Oh, Joey," he sighed, surrendering yet again to the power this small female held over his heart.

He took her into his arms as the sun set behind the trees, not caring if it ever rose again, if he couldn't face that sunrise with Joey by his side. She was nothing that he had been looking for, if indeed he had been looking for anything, but she was all that he ever wanted. All that he ever needed. She had driven into his life and into his heart. And he would never let her go.

She wasn't as independent as Roseanne, but she was definitely more free. She wasn't as helplessly feminine as Muffy, but she was more than enough female for him to handle. She wasn't as *Ursula* as Ursula, but then no one was—or even should be. She wasn't immensely talented, like Courtney Blackmun, but who wanted the hassle of living with a temperamental writer, anyway? Not him, that was for sure. Never again.

No, Joey wasn't anything like Roseanne, or Muffy, or Ursula, or Courtney. More important, she was light-years away from anything Veronica had been.

She was Joey. Just Joey. Loving, kind and giving Joey. Free-spirited, generous, optimistic Joey, without a single selfish, self-interested bone in her body. She gave without question, and accepted without tying strings around him. And he loved her.

His mouth buried against the curve of her neck, his hands freely roving over previously unexplored territory as she nibbled at his ear, Daniel felt his body rock with shock at his last thought.

He loved her.

Daniel Quinn loved Joey Abbott.

"How about that!" His hands stilled in the act of creeping beneath her loose cotton tank top. Slowly, as a smile slid onto his face, he lifted his head to look deeply into her eyes. "I'm in love with you," he said, and she could hear the laughter in his voice.

"And that's funny?" she asked him, her heart suddenly pounding even faster than it had been ever since he'd lifted her onto the bench. "You have a perverted sense of humor, Daniel. I think you ought to know that."

"Why? I'm a reasonably normal man, respected in my field, who has gone and fallen in love with a half-pint, bigmouthed, baseball-playing, purple sneaker-wearing chauffeur who used to be a computer executive and full-time vagabond. Oh, yes. Did I forget to mention that her brother wants to be a rock star with his own MTV video? All in all, I'd say it's very funny."

"And I've fallen in love with a big-shot New York publisher who only learned to laugh ten minutes ago, and who has a whiz kid son, a kooky housekeeper who

keeps bringing her dead husband into the conversation and a father-in-law who thinks he's Peter Pan.
You're no bargain, Daniel Quinn. Just remember that.
Now, the question remains—what are we going to do
about it?''

Daniel kissed the tip of her nose. ''About what? Richie? Peter Pan? I refuse to take lifelong responsibility
for Mrs. Hemmings, no matter how much my son likes
her chocolate chip cookies.''

''Forget the cookies. I mean, what are we going to
do about the fact that we love each other,'' Joey reminded him, pressing her forehead against his.

Joey watched, amazed, as Daniel's face rearranged
itself into a leer. ''Well, I can think of one thing. But
we'd have to dump the kid first.''

Batting her eyelashes furiously, Joey gasped, asking, ''Why *Danny*, whatever do you mean?''

''Hey, you guys!'' Richie's voice came booming out
at them from beneath the wooden porch roof, so that
Joey, startled, nearly tumbled from the bench onto the
grass. ''I've got it. I know I've got it. I have to get right
home and feed it into my computer.''

''He's got it,'' Daniel said quietly as he steadied Joey
on the bench.

''Bully for him,'' Joey commented fatalistically,
knowing the mood had been broken. ''Let's just hope
it's not catching. I think you'd better let go now, Daniel, I'm not going to fall.''

Richie ran down the steps onto the lawn, then
stopped, suddenly realizing that his father and Joey

were locked in each other's arms. "Hey, what are you two guys doing, anyhow?"

"And to think he used to be so articulate," Daniel mused in mock sorrow, releasing Joey reluctantly.

"And much more perceptive," Joey agreed, brushing down her clothes while trying to recover her composure, "not that I think it's going to take him too long to catch on. You'd better help me down before he starts giving us chapter and verse from his last sex education class."

Within ten minutes the three of them had succeeded in clearing up the remnants of their cookout. Richie had run ahead to get in Daniel's car, his father lingering behind only long enough to arrange for Joey to pick up Courtney in the morning and steal one last, unsatisfying kiss.

"I could send him to summer camp," he suggested, not wanting to let her go. "As a matter of fact, I'd even consider sending him to Wilbur for a few weeks. Joey, you're looking at a desperate man!"

She shook her head. "Only if you can send Andy along with him. Remember, he comes home tomorrow. That's two strikes, Daniel—with both of our houses out of the running. You'll have to come up with another idea."

He leaned down for one last kiss. "Give me time. I'll think of something," he promised, and then he was gone.

Joey fell asleep that night with a smile on her face, to dream that her father and mother were in the bedroom with her, silently giving her their blessing.

Joey didn't recognize the Courtney Blackmun that walked out the front door early the next morning, dragging one of her own suitcases behind her. She was wearing well-worn jeans and a thin cotton top that hung down to her thighs, and her glorious black hair was tied back haphazardly in a ponytail. Her face, still beautiful, was free of makeup, and she was wearing bright green high-top sneakers.

"Wilbur would be appalled," Joey said under her breath as she got out of the limousine in order to relieve Courtney of the suitcase. "Good morning, Ms. Blackmun," she called out, moving across the driveway at a near run. "Let me get that for you."

"No need, Joey," the writer responded, hefting the suitcase down the steps. "And please, the name is Courtney. Richie is bringing the other two, if he can tear himself away from Mrs. Hemmings's heavenly blueberry pancakes. I came out ahead of him to have a cigarette. Mrs. Hemmings frowns upon them, you know."

"There have been rumors to that effect," Joey sympathized, opening the trunk. "But where's Daniel? He's usually an early riser." She looked around, expecting him to appear at any moment. Needing him to appear, so that she could look into his eyes and believe that yesterday had been real and not just some wonderful, wishful dream.

Richie came stumbling out the door, nearly lost beneath the weight and bulk of one overnight case and the large Gucci bag. "Dad's on the phone with London, Joey, and says you're to go on without him but come straight back here. Oh, yeah, and you're to drive carefully. Do you want me to kiss you goodbye instead?" he finished, making puckering motions with his mouth.

"You'll do five laps before the game this afternoon for that one, buster," Joey warned him, ruffling his hair as he passed her on the way to the trunk. "And tell your father I *always* drive carefully. Courtney?" she prompted, holding open the door to the backseat.

Courtney shook her head. "I'd much rather ride up front with you, if you don't mind the cigarette smoke. I don't think I'm dressed for all that opulence back there."

The woman was full of surprises, Joey thought, shutting the passenger door and gesturing toward the front of the limousine. "Esmeralda and I would be honored to have you."

Courtney settled herself into the front seat, fastening her lap and shoulder belt and promptly lighting a cigarette. "All right," she said, exhaling a long stream of smoke, "let's have it. How serious is this thing between you and Daniel?"

Her question had surprised Joey, but she answered it honestly. "Very serious, at least on my part. I'm in love with the guy."

"He's been hurt. But you already know that, don't you?"

"Veronica. His late wife," Joey answered solemnly, nodding her head. "Daniel told me about it. It was all very sad."

"It was all very criminal," Courtney declared, "and all because of a book."

"A book?" Joey averted her eyes from the road for a moment to sneak a look in Courtney's direction, trying to understand. "I think I've lost you. Daniel told me she was killed in a plane crash. How could a book have anything to do with that?"

Courtney settled herself more comfortably in her seat and lit another cigarette. "I have to quit these things before they kill me," she said, holding the cigarette in front of her and glaring at it. "I've quit at least a dozen times, only to start again when an idea hits me. I'm going to do a three-generational saga this time, ending with the bombing of Nagasaki."

"Courtney," Joey prompted, not caring that she was being told something the rest of the world wouldn't know for another two years, "you opened this particular can of worms. Now finish it."

The writer stubbed out the cigarette, breaking its length in two in the ashtray. "Filthy habit. All right, Joey, I'll agree that the marriage was doomed from the beginning. Veronica was beautiful, but she was spoiled rotten. Wilbur saw to that, bless his heart. He meant well. Men always *mean* well."

"I like Wilbur," Joey warned stiffly.

"Who doesn't like him?" Courtney countered, popping a breath mint into her mouth. "Wilbur's a pussycat. I really believe Daniel married Veronica because he liked Wilbur so much, even if they have been playing tug-of-war with Richie this past year or so. Daniel didn't need to marry the boss's daughter, you know. He's the best in the business, or I would have jumped ship years ago. In publishing, loyalty is nothing but a seven-letter word meaning 'make me an offer I can't refuse.'"

Joey was silent, trying to remember to concentrate on the traffic as they crossed the Phillipsburg Bridge into New Jersey.

"It could have been a civilized divorce, if it hadn't been for the book. Veronica fancied herself to be a writer, you understand." Courtney turned to look at Joey, shaking her head as she made a face. "Bad," she said, shivering with distaste. "Very, *very* bad."

"But she wanted Daniel to publish it?" Joey questioned, a lump vaguely resembling a rock the size of Gibraltar forming in her stomach.

"Why not? Wilbur had published the first one." Once again, Courtney turned to Joey. "*Badder* than bad," she intoned gravely. "It was Veronica's version of the Civil *Wa-ar, dahling*. Wilbur bought up all the copies and sent them overseas to some needy country that didn't have any books of their own. I think they sent them back. Daniel told her he wouldn't publish her second effort. Veronica, well—Veronica didn't take rejection well."

Joey thought she was going to be sick. "What did she do?"

The jeweled cigarette lighter snapped closed and Courtney expelled another thin white stream of smoke. "She punished him, of course. She took lovers—quite openly. She tried to drive a wedge between Wilbur and Daniel. She neglected her son, bad-mouthed her husband to anyone who would listen and finally got herself killed in that plane crash before Daniel could work up the courage to strangle her. No writer's had a snowball's chance in hell of getting close to him ever since. No female writer, that is. He's a good one, Joey, don't let him get away. I don't believe in gossip, but I like you, which is why I told you all this. Not that you're writing a book, right?''

Joey laughed weakly. ''Right!'' she said, wanting to crawl off somewhere and die.

Chapter Ten

Joey's mind was racing out of control as she headed back down the New Jersey Turnpike, racing toward Pennsylvania. Why had she ever shown her manuscript to Wilbur? Why hadn't she just kept on submitting the darn thing over the transom, like any other unpublished writer? Why hadn't she just tried to get a literary agent, and let him handle it? Why had she ever written the damn thing in the first place?

Had she sworn Wilbur to secrecy? No, of course she hadn't. That would have been too obvious, too intelligent, too *normal*. No, she had just handed the thing to him, and asked him to give his honest opinion.

An honest opinion? From Wilbur Langley? The man who looked at her and saw her as the answer to all his prayers for making Daniel and Richie into a family again? The same man who had published his daughter's book when it was "badder than bad"?

Whom had she been kidding? Of course, Wilbur was going to like her manuscript. The man liked twelve-foot-long blood-red lips on his walls, for crying out loud! When it came to women—daughters, prospective daughters-in-law or pretty women who appealed to him—Wilbur Langley had about as much objectivity as a three-year-old set loose in a toy store.

She'd been out to have her ego stroked, that was what she'd done. Oh, she could have talked herself into believing that she had only wanted Wilbur's opinion because his approval of her work would also justify her leaving Ransom Computers and wandering the country for two years like some gypsy. After all, Daniel had condemned her life-style. She had been looking for justification of her life, her reason for existing.

"And I wanted to know if I was talented," she admitted out loud, so that the tolltaker on the Phillipsburg Bridge looked at her warily as she drove away. "I wanted to have someone pat me on the back and say I was this decade's answer to J. D. Salinger."

Her foot rode the gas pedal heavily as she tooled Esmeralda down the thruway, hoping against hope that Wilbur's doorman was wrong, and the retired publisher had not left town that morning to visit his grandson "in the wilds of Pennsylvania."

Why had Wilbur decided to visit today, of all days? Maybe he hadn't had time to read her manuscript. It was possible. Anything was possible.

Maybe, even if he *had* read it, he wouldn't have shown it to Daniel. Because, she thought grimly as she pulled Esmeralda into the Quinn driveway, if he ever did show it to Daniel her world would be over.

Mrs. Hemmings opened the front door for her, shaking her head as she informed her that Daniel and Richie had already left for the Bulldogs' baseball game, but Mr. Wilbur was there if she wanted to see him. "A very nice man, Mr. Wilbur," the housekeeper remarked as she led the way to the living room, "but he's a bit strange. He kept turning the lights on and off, saying he didn't know we had such conveniences in Pennsylvania."

Joey smiled at Mrs. Hemmings's obvious confusion and relaxed a bit. She had forgotten all about the baseball game. Maybe there was still time to save herself. "Just don't forget to take him around back to show him the little house with the half-moon on the door," she advised just as Wilbur came into the foyer, his arms outstretched in greeting.

"Darling Joey!" he exclaimed, taking hold of both her hands and bringing them to his lips. "At last someone has shown up to greet me. Daniel and my grandson are nowhere to be found. Why didn't you tell me you were so vastly talented? I wept as I read your brilliant manuscript, I tell you. Wept and laughed, and sighed deep, satisfied sighs."

"You laughed, you cried, it became a part of you," Joey recited dully, not believing him for a minute. "You didn't show it to Daniel, did you?"

"Daniel?" Wilbur repeated, looking puzzled as he sat on the sofa facing the chair she had dropped into, exhausted. "Why should I show it to Daniel? You're my coup, not his. Let him discover his own genius. You're mine. I want to edit you personally."

"Edit me?" Joey repeated, too relieved to fully take in what Wilbur was saying.

He leaned across the coffee table to pat her hand. "Did you think I completely walked away, my dear? I still dabble in the company occasionally, taking care of my own select list of authors. One of them is on the bestseller list right now. I think you might know of her. Courtney Blackmun?"

Joey's eyes nearly popped out of her head. "You edit Courtney Blackmun? Wilbur, I'm impressed!"

He leaned back in his seat. "Don't be, my dear. She only allows me a bit of comma movement here and there, and an occasional minor correction of syntax. Courtney's a law unto herself at Langley Books. But she's not my only author. And now I have you. Congratulations, Joey Abbott, and welcome to my stable. Stable—as if writers were horses."

Joey shook her head, first slowly, and then quickly, vehemently in the negative. "No, Wilbur," she told him fiercely. "I can't, honestly. I can't let Daniel know I've written a book. He'll think I was only using him in order to get published. It's not like I was planning a career as a writer. I just wrote it, that's all. Maybe in a couple of years I'll consider it again, but for now—"

Wilbur's brow furrowed as he considered this new thought. "But that's ridiculous. If you were using him, then why didn't you give the manuscript directly to him, instead of to me?"

She jumped to her feet, spreading her hands. "Because I was using him to get to you, of course!" she blurted, knowing she was in danger of becoming hysterical. "Maybe I was even using Richie in order to get to either one of you. Who knows what he'll think! Courtney says—"

"Courtney?" Wilbur repeated, cutting her off as he rose to put his arm around her. "Lovely girl, Courtney. She told you about Veronica, didn't she? I'm sure she meant well. Courtney is never mean. But I see why you're upset. Have you considered a pen name? *One for the Road* must be put in print. It would be a crime to hide it because you're afraid of what Daniel might think."

"Oh, Wilbur!" Joey groaned, laying her head against his silk-shirted chest. "What a fine mess I've gotten myself into this time!"

Joey went home without seeing Daniel, knowing that Andy had arrived back in town that afternoon and would be wondering why his loving sister hadn't been there to greet him. He'd also be wondering where his dinner was, she thought fatalistically, knowing that there was no problem so big that it couldn't be pushed into the background long enough to satisfy Andy's enormous appetite.

The Mercedes was gone when she pulled into the driveway in front of the house, and a note propped against the salt shaker on the kitchen table told her that

Andy had gone to see the Bulldogs play, hoping to find her there. Shrugging her shoulders, she decided to start dinner, knowing he would be home soon, three hot-dogs under his belt, and still ravenous. Besides, it would pass the time until Daniel was to pick her up for their prearranged dinner date.

Andy came barreling through the door just as the kitchen timer signaled that the spaghetti noodles were al dente, grabbing his sister in a bear hug that lifted her completely off the floor. "Hi, Sis!" he shouted into her ear. "Boy, that smells good. Miss me?"

"Did Fay Wray miss King Kong? Did Tarzan miss Cheetah? Put me down, you big ape, before the spa-ghetti gets all mushy. Let me look at you. Is it possi-ble? It looks like you've grown. What did you bring me?"

Andy turned a kitchen chair around and straddled it. "Just like a kid—'what did you bring me, Daddy?' I got you a turquoise necklace from this really neat In-dian reservation we visited, but it's still in my suitcase. I'll unpack after dinner, okay?"

"Squash?"

"Squash? I thought we were having spaghetti and meatballs. I hate squash."

Joey pretended to hit him with the colander as she prepared to drain the spaghetti. "Not squash. *Squash.* Is it a squash necklace?"

Andy shrugged, reaching into the salad bowl in the middle of the table to extract a slice of cucumber. "Darned if I know. It's blue. Hey, what's with Mr. Quinn? He used to have a sense of humor."

Pausing in the middle of pouring the spaghetti into the colander, Joey turned her head to correct her brother's mistaken impression. "Daniel's got a wonderful sense of humor. You just can't tell a joke, brother mine. I've told you that before. Just keep practicing on that guitar. It's the only hope you've got."

The telephone rang and Andy hopped up to answer it. He said hello, and then just listened. Hanging it up a few moments later, he straddled the chair once more and said, "That was Mr. Quinn. He says he has to cancel your date for tonight. Something about having his father-in-law in town and having to catch up on some work he's been neglecting. He sounded strange." Andy popped another cucumber slice into his mouth.

Joey looked down at the amount of cooked spaghetti, knowing there wasn't enough for her, as she had thought she was going out for dinner. It didn't matter, because she had suddenly lost her appetite. Numbly, her hands moving automatically, she set the food in front of her brother and then sat down before she fell down.

He couldn't know. It was ridiculous. Wilbur wasn't going to tell him. He was going to leave that up to her. He'd promised, under the pain of forfeiting his lifelong membership at the Metropolitan Museum. It had to have been Andy, ridiculous and horrible as that seemed.

"Andy," she asked carefully as he twirled some spaghetti around his fork and popped it into his mouth, "what made you think Daniel has no sense of humor? What joke did you tell him?"

Waiting until Andy was done chewing and swallowing was almost more than she could bear. "I didn't tell him a joke, Sis," he said at last. "Well, not an *actual* joke. I was talking to him between innings—we won by the way—and I just asked him what he thought of your book."

"You asked him what he thought of my book?" Joey squeaked, closing her eyes, and leaning her forehead on her hand. "Oh, Andy, how could you?"

"What do you mean, how could I? You told me on the phone that he's some sort of publisher. Why shouldn't I ask him? I mean, you're my sister, and I know you. You wouldn't let an opportunity like that pass you by."

"But just in case I had, you were going to do my dirty work for me, right? Go on," she said tightly.

"Yeah, well, there's not much more to tell. I just asked him if he got a good laugh out of your spelling. I may not have read your book, but I do read your trip log. You've got to be the only person in the world who spells New Jersey with a *G*. Anyway, Daniel didn't think it was funny—the G business, you know. He just looked at me in this goofy way and then went back out to coach first base. Do I drive him tomorrow, or do you?"

Remembering Daniel's earlier order—given in anger, but given just the same—that Andy take over the job of chauffeuring him as soon as he got back from vacation, Joey said, "You do," and then fled from the kitchen before her brother could see the tears she could no longer hide. It was all over. Daniel hated her. He had every right to hate her. She hadn't been honest with him. And now it was too late for anything except regret.

Daniel was unsurprised to see Andy behind the wheel when Esmeralda's gleaming white body pulled up in front of the door the next morning. Wilbur, standing beside him, leaned closer to him and gibed, "Not that I'm the sort to say 'I told you so,' but—I told you so! To use the vernacular, you blew it, buster."

"Thank you for those words of wisdom, Wilbur," Daniel replied tersely. "Now why don't you go crawl into your bed before the sun comes up?"

Wilbur stepped back a pace, clutching a hand to his chest. "Ah! You got me! I'm cut to the quick. But the question remains—what are you going to do about my favorite author?"

"Courtney Blackmun?" Daniel asked, avoiding the question. "What should I do with her? She's tucked up in her Manhattan apartment, puffing and creating. You should be doing handsprings. I know I am."

"Not that favorite author. I mean Joey," Wilbur corrected, unruffled. "What are you going to do about dearest Joey?"

Daniel's head snapped around as he confronted his father-in-law. "Joey's *my* author, if she'll let me within ten feet of her work."

Wilbur smiled and corrected, "On the contrary, old son. I discovered her. Joey's mine."

Andy had apparently heard enough. Letting go of the passenger door he'd been holding open, he approached the men. "Why don't you just cut her in half? Then you can both have some of her."

Wilbur looked down at Andy. "This is the brother, I presume. He's as tall as she's small, isn't he?" He held out his hand. "Andrew? You're the aspiring singer, isn't that correct? If you can sing as well as your sister can write, I may have a theatrical agent for you. I believe he once had something to do with a lad named Spring-something-or-other."

Daniel watched in knowing resignation as Andy, formerly angry for his sister's sake and ready to take on the world to defend her, turned into a smiling tower of jelly at Wilbur's words. "And another one bites the dust," he spit in disgust, heading for the limousine. "Come on, Andy, I've got places to go and people to see."

"You shouldn't be going to the city, Daniel," Wilbur called after him. "You should be crawling over to Joey's house—preferably on your knees."

"I'll handle this my own way, and in my own time, thank you. Goodbye, Wilbur," Daniel called over his shoulder as he bent his tall frame in order to enter the backseat. "Try not to corrupt Mrs. Hemmings while I'm gone."

"I can't do it."

"Of course you can, Sis. We've got nothing else on for tonight," Andy said, chasing his retreating sister from the kitchen out onto the porch.

She threw herself onto the porch swing and began rocking it back and forth furiously. "All right then, Andy, I *won't* do it. Is that better? And what is he up to, coming back from New York this early in the day?" She glared up at her brother. "Did he bring someone named Ursula with him?" she asked suspiciously.

Andy shook his head. "He was alone. Now look, Joey, it's only a trip to Stokesay Castle. You've made the trip five dozen times. Why not tonight?"

She crossed her arms tightly against her breast and continued to rock the old swing back and forth at a dangerously fast rate. "Because I wouldn't cross the street with Daniel Quinn, that's why. I'm not about to chauffeur him and his latest dinner companion to Reading. I didn't contract out for that."

Leaning against the wooden porch rail, Andy lifted a hand to scratch at a spot just above his left ear, a clear warning sign that he was about to say something she didn't want to hear. The last time he'd scratched that spot he had told her he wanted to be a rock star. "I'm not contracted out for that—am I, Andy?" she asked, jamming her feet against the porch to stop the swing.

"Well, ac-tu-ally—" Andy began warily.

"Andrew Abbott, what have you gotten me into?" she shrieked, remembering that Andy had been the one to sign the contract. Why hadn't she taken the time to read it before gaily delivering it to the loan officer at the bank like a Christmas pudding? "Andrew—speak to me!"

Andy took a deep breath and began talking fast. "The contract says that Daniel has first dibs at our service for the length of the contract. It says that he is to have the driver of his choice, and that the contract is null and void if we fail to deliver without adequate explanation of our inability to perform. So that's why we have to transport Daniel to Stokesay Castle tonight for his dinner date, and that's why you have to drive him. If we don't, we blow the contract. You said the guy from the bank called today to say we have the loan, so we can't lose Daniel now or else we'll lose the whole ball game. Right?'' he ended, lifting his hands as if to ward off physical attack.

Joey's next words were spoken very slowly. ''I think I'm going to be ill. Seriously ill.''

Andy lowered his hands. ''But you'll do it?''

''I'll do it,'' she answered, rising to her feet with all the dignity of a French aristocrat about to face the guillotine. ''But he's going to regret it. *Boy*, is he going to regret it!''

''He's a nice guy, Sis. Why do you hate him?'' Andy asked as Joey headed for the kitchen door.

''Because it's easier than the alternative,'' she replied, her answer totally lost on Andy, who wasn't a woman in love, and couldn't understand.

Stokesay Castle was always beautiful, but this warm summer night it was exquisite, sitting atop its own slice of the mountain, its turrets catching the last lingering rays of the setting sun, its gray stone walls and mullioned windows looking warm and inviting. It was a place constructed out of love, and with a loving eye to detail, from the large, dark wood-paneled entranceway to the dining rooms hung with full-size portraits and heavy tapestries.

No matter how many times Joey made the trip, bringing lovers here for the perfect setting for "popping the question" over specially prepared dinners, and happily married couples celebrating their anniversaries, the castle remained special to Joey.

That was why she had regretted telling Daniel about it in the first place, for he had brought Roseanne here, and Muffy, but never her. And that was why she was dying by inches now as she tooled Esmeralda along the twisting roadway that led to the restaurant.

It had been a silent drive, with Daniel sitting alone in the back of the limousine, looking perfectly wonderful in his dark suit, and completely remote, with his hands crossed against his chest. He had been waiting for her when she pulled into the drive, and helped himself into the backseat, a single curt nod of his head motioning her to proceed to Reading.

It took forty-five minutes to reach the castle, long, heartbreaking minutes during which Joey's mood rocketed back and forth between anger and the faint, wild glimmerings of hope. After all, he was alone. Was he meeting someone? Was this to be the moment he would unveil the famous Ursula? Or was he sitting back there struggling with his conscience, trying to find some way to make up for breaking her heart?

Surely he knew her heart was broken. It didn't take a computer whiz to figure out that he had learned about *One for the Road* and immediately jumped to all the wrong conclusions.

No, she decided at least three times between Kutz-
town and the outskirts of Reading, *he isn't planning
some cute, silly, romantic way to apologize. He's doing
this deliberately, riding in splendor while I sit up front,
my stupid cap on my stupid head, his paid lackey. He's
just putting me back in my place—firmly. I could kill
him! I love him so much!*

"Your driving wasn't quite as smooth as usual,
Joey," Daniel remarked blandly as he exited the limousine, having waited almost a full five minutes for her
to climb out of the front seat and stomp around to the
other side to open his door.

"Be happy I didn't run you off the cliff," she answered from between compressed lips, watching as he
entered the restaurant without looking at her. She
waited until the door closed behind him, standing at
attention until she was sure it was safe to release her
pent-up breath. "And now, Mr. Daniel Quinn, I hope
you enjoy your dinner. I hope you enjoy it because it's
going to be a long walk back to Saucon Valley!"

She was just about to strap on her seat belt, her fingers fumbling with the need to be away from the restaurant before she could change her mind, when one of
the waitresses knocked on the windshield. "Hi, Joey,"
she said, motioning for her to lower the window.
"Come on inside. I have something to show you."

"Not tonight, Ginny," Joey pleaded. "I really have
to be going. Some other—"

"But it's the neatest thing! You've got to see it, Joey.
It's up on the roof—on top of the tower. Come on. It'll
just take a minute."

Joey sighed, removing the key from the ignition. "What is it, Ginny?" she asked, following the waitress into the restaurant. "Have you finally figured out where Elvis has been hiding himself all these years? Has he taken up residence in the secret room in the tower? Have you looked in the dungeon lately—maybe Buddy Holly is down there."

Ginny, a devoted rock and roll fan, laughed nervously. "Don't be silly," she admonished, taking Joey's hand and leading her up the winding staircase that led to the top of the tower. "The owners have decided to fix up an outdoor eating area for young lovers up here and I knew you'd want to see it so you could tell your clients about it. Hey, Joey, you remember that couple you brought down last year—the guy who had me put the engagement ring in his girlfriend's champagne glass? They were back last week for their first anniversary. She's going to have a baby just before Christmas! Isn't that sweet?"

"Adorable," Joey agreed, wondering why fate had chosen a nice girl like Ginny to drive a stake through her heart. She tried to change the subject. "How will you get the food all the way up here before it gets cold?"

"A dumbwaiter, dummy," Ginny answered with a smile, opening the door at the top of the stairs and then standing back to motion for Joey to precede her.

Joey took two steps onto the flat, parapet-ringed roof before the door slammed shut behind her. She whirled about, calling out to Ginny, then froze as a male voice said, "I thought you'd never get here. Come over here and sit down. Your onion soup is getting cold."

She didn't turn around, but only stared at the closed door. "Daniel," she said, closing her eyes, trying desperately not to betray herself by breaking down.

"One and the same," he acknowledged, walking over to place his hands on her shoulders. "It was a juvenile idea, but the best one I could come up with to get you alone."

"I suppose there's really a table set for dinner up here for us?" she asked, still refusing to turn around.

"There is," he told her, rubbing his hands up and down her arms. "I've ordered filet mignon for you. I'm having a large serving of humble pie for my main course."

"Because you were angry when Andy told you I'd written a book?"

"No, my darling Joey. Because I was *stupid* when Andy told me you'd written a book. Stupid, and temporarily insane. You'd never try to use me to get a book published. You're entirely too honest to do something like that. I should have known that immediately. Especially not to publish a book like *One for the Road*."

Now she did turn around. It was the "darling" that did it. The "darling" and the way his voice had softened when he mentioned the title of her book. "You read it?" She looked up at him, her gray eyes wide with the unspoken question: Did you like it?

His hands tightening on her shoulders, he smiled and nodded that he had. "It's a curiously naive, yet comforting look at the people of this country through the eyes of someone just discovering life. Youth and innocence shine through every word, Joey. Your youth, your innocence."

She swallowed down hard on the sudden lump in her throat. "You laughed, you cried, it became a part of you," she joked feebly, her bottom lip trembling as tears threatened to spill down her cheeks.

"I'm tossing Wilbur for the chance to edit it—and all the books you're going to write. Best two out of three falls wins," Daniel told her as his finger came up to gently wipe away one traitorous tear. "If you'll let me?"

"Just try to weasel your way out of it, buster!" she warned, putting her hands against his chest, just to be sure he was real. And he was real, real and solid, and more wonderful than ever.

His next words proved it. "I love you, Josephine Abbott. Please, for my sake, and Richie's sake, and even, God help me, Wilbur's sake, will you marry me, Josephine?"

She answered him with her kiss, never even noticing that he had called her Josephine.

*   *   *   *   *

COMING NEXT MONTH

#706 NEVER ON SUNDAE—Rita Rainville
A Diamond Jubilee Title!
Heather Brandon wanted to help women lose weight. But lean, hard
Wade Mackenzie had different ideas. He wanted Heather to lose her
heart—to him!

#707 DOMESTIC BLISS—Karen Leabo
By working as a maid, champion of women's rights Spencer Guthrie
tried to prove he practiced what he preached. But could he convince
tradition-minded Bonnie Chapman that he loved a woman like her?

#708 THE MARK OF ZORRO—Samantha Grey
Once conservative Sarah Wingate saw "the man in the mask" she
couldn't keep her thoughts on co-worker Jeff Baxter. But then she
learned he and Zorro were one and the same!

#709 A CHILD CALLED MATTHEW—Sara Grant
Laura Bryant was determined to find her long-lost son at any cost.
Then she discovered the key to the mystery lay with Gareth Ryder, the
man who had once broken her heart.

#710 TIGER BY THE TAIL—Pat Tracy
Sarah Burke had grown up among tyrants, so Lucas Rockworth's
gentle demeanor drew her like a magnet. Soon, however, she learned
her lamb roared like a lion!

#711 SEALED WITH A KISS—Joan Smith
Impetuous Jodie James was off with stuffy—but handsome!—Greg
Edison to look for their missing brothers. Jodie knew they were a
mismatched couple, but she was starting to believe the old adage that
opposites attract....

AVAILABLE THIS MONTH:

**#700 THE AMBASSADOR'S
DAUGHTER**
Brittany Young

#701 HIS CHARIOT AWAITS
Kasey Michaels

#702 BENEATH SIERRA SKIES
Shannon Gale

#703 A LIBERATED MAN
Diana Whitney

#704 SO EASY TO LOVE
Marcy Gray

#705 A PERFECT GENTLEMAN
Arlene James